What Teachers, Parents and Students are Saying about

MYSTERY ON RAMPART HILL

"The *Rocky Mountain Mysteries* are delightful mystery novels that my daughter and I enjoy reading together. It's not often you find adventures like these that will stimulate conversation between parent and child. We recommend these wonderful mysteries for every youth's library."
— Bridgette (Parent) & Alexandra, 11 years old Centennial, Colorado

"I recommend this book because it has great details, and you can picture what the Author is saying."
— Camia, 8 years old.

"Mystery on Rampart Hill was fun to read. It kept my interest, and I was surprised about how it ended."
— Josh, 12 years old.

"My favorite part of the book was when they find the key to the old trunk."
— Nicole, 12 years old.

"I love this book and the best thing about it is that a boy & a girl went on this adventure!"
— 6th grader Denver Public Schools

More of What People are saying

"These books are fabulous! My step son and I spend special times together reading them every time he comes to visit. We are sharing these great adventures, learning more about places in Colorado and becoming such good friends."
— Hollie &
Ronny, 10 years old

"This was a fun book and even better (more funner) because it was about our state and it made the story feel more real."
— 6th grader
Denver Public Schools

"The Colorado roots first attracted me to this book. The adventure itself kept me in it. The students in my classes loved it!"
— Nancy
Denver Public School Teacher
Educational Consultant & Instructor
Colorado Consulting
University of Phoenix,
Denver Campus

Rocky Mountain Mysteries™

MYSTERY ON RAMPART HILL

Emily Burns

Illustrated By
John Breeding

Covered Wagon Publishing LLC

ROCKY MOUNTAIN MYSTERIES: 1
    MYSTERY ON RAMPART HILL

ISBN: 0-9723259-0-5

10 9 8 7 6 5 4 3 2 First Printing: November 2002

Printed in the United States of America by:
    United Graphics Incorporated
    2916 Marshall Ave · Mattoon, Il 61938
    Cover printed on 10PT C1S- Bright white cover with lay-flat gloss laminate.
    Interior pages printed on $60^{\#}$ offset

Published and distributed by

                        Covered Wagon Publishing, LLC,
                        PO Box 473038 Aurora, Colorado 80047-3038.
                        jackd@coveredwagonpublishing.com

Library of Congress Control Number: 2002112437

Illustrated by John Breeding

Book Design, Cover Design and Art Direction by
        A. J. Images Inc.
        Communication & Graphic Design
        www.ajimagesinc.com – 303·696·9227

For educational and individual sales information,
call Covered Wagon Publishing, 1.303.751.0992
Visit our web site at: http://www.RockyMountainMysteries.com

Acknowledgements

A special thanks to Karin Hoffman, A. J. Images, Inc., for the time that she has spent helping us put this book together. We appreciate her talent and expertise as well as the sincere interest that she has given us. We would also like to thank our illustrator, John Breeding. We feel truly blessed to be working with someone so talented. Thanks to our grandparents, along with Barbara and Emily, for assisting in the editing of this book.

We want to also thank the teachers and kids who were the first to read this book and share their insight with us. Your interest in this book and upcoming books is very inspirational, and it is what keeps us going.

Dedicated to my father, who taught me
the meaning of hard work and dedication;
to my husband, Jack, who has always believed
in me; and to Grandma and Grandpa for
their support and editing assistance.

Tyler -

is sixteen years old and has brown hair and brown eyes. His hobbies include camping, fishing, baseball, and white water rafting. His best friend is Dylan.

Dylan -

is sixteen years old with reddish/brown hair. He is on the high school football team and enjoys fishing, watching movies, and hanging out with his friends.

Stephanie -

is fourteen years old and a twin to her brother, Steve. She enjoys reading, writing, and playing the piano. Stephanie's best friend is Kamryn.

Kamryn -

is thirteen years old with blond hair and blue eyes. Her hobbies include shopping, music, reading, the drama club, playing games, and bike riding.

Steve -

has light brown hair and hazel eyes like his twin sister. His favorite pastime is baseball. He enjoys reading, camping, photography, and fishing. His best friend is Andrew.

Andrew -

is thirteen years old with brown hair and brown eyes. His hobbies include wrestling, baseball, swimming, and collecting trading cards.

Contents

Chapter 1
The Angry Roar

"I heard that it's haunted," fourteen-year-old Steve said, as he walked in the back door with his twin sister, Stephanie.

"Kamryn used to walk by it with her dog, Scamper, until she started seeing lights flicker and hearing strange noises inside," Stephanie said referring to her best friend.

As the twins entered the large country kitchen in their house, they saw their mother getting dinner ready. They washed their hands and started setting the table.

"What's all this talk about haunted houses?" Carol Thompson asked her son and daughter.

Stephanie, who was very outspoken, was the first to tell her mother the good news about the new library being built. Finally, the Thompson kids, who lived on the outskirts of the small town of Buena Vista, Colorado, would have a library closer to their home. As Stephanie told her mother the details about the library, their yellow lab, Sammy, was barking outside. It was not like Stephanie and Steve to ignore her, and she wanted their attention.

"A new library sounds great, but what does this have to do with a haunted house?" Mrs. Thompson asked Stephanie impatiently.

"There is a rumor going around that the library site is haunted," Stephanie explained to her mother as her older brother, Tyler, walked in the door.

"Hey, I think you guys hurt Sammy's feelings," he said as he rubbed their cat, Lucky. "He looked up so sadly when I walked past him."

"Sorry, we were just telling Mom about the new library," Steve said. "The town just bought that run-down house on Rampart Hill to fix up for a new library."

"A lot of the kids are talking about the house being haunted," Stephanie added.

"Surely you guys don't believe in haunted houses," Tyler teased his younger brother and sister.

"Of course not," Steve answered, and then added, "but there is no explanation for some of the things that have been happening."

"Like what?" Tyler asked.

"Some of my friends have seen flickering lights and shadowy figures through the windows," Steve said.

"Shadows through what windows?" their father, Jack Thompson, asked as he walked in the door.

"That old house up on Rampart Hill," Carol Thompson answered for them. "Kids, you can tell your father all about the house and the library after we sit down to dinner."

After the family said grace, the twins filled their father in on the new "haunted" library. Stephanie asked her father if he knew anything about the house.

"That house was there long before we moved here," he told his children. "I remember driving by it when we were looking for land to build this house, and I'm pretty sure that someone was living there then. Stephanie, you were only about ten so that must have been about four years ago."

Stephanie remembered when her family had moved from Westminster, a suburb of Denver. Even though she had to leave many friends behind, Stephanie was happy to move away from the hectic city life. Before they moved, her father had been a history teacher and her mother had worked as a part-time real estate agent. They became interested in writing travel articles for magazines. Soon, they had a steady flow of assignments from several major magazines. It was about a year after that when they started building their house in the foothills near Buena Vista, a peaceful, rural area in the middle of the Colorado Rocky Mountains.

"Our lives have really changed," Mrs. Thompson commented.

After washing the dishes and cleaning up the kitchen, the three teenagers sat at the breakfast table to work on their homework assignments. Later in the evening, they said good night to their parents, and they each went upstairs to their bedrooms. The boys, who had always shared a room before moving to their new house, were especially thankful that they each had their own room. Tyler liked to watch television before falling asleep while Steve liked to read. The funny thing was that after years of complaining about sharing a room they hardly ever went directly to their own rooms.

"There's a good movie on tonight," Tyler told his brother. "Do you want to watch it with me?"

"Sure," Steve said, following him into his room.

Stephanie went to her own room decorated with lavender flower wallpaper and a white-laced bedspread. As she curled up in her bed with the book she had recently started reading, she heard a scratching at her door. She opened the door for Lucky, who purred as he curled up next to her. Soon they were both fast asleep.

The next day at school their English teacher, Mrs. Adams, told the class about a book drive to collect books for the new library.

"Whoever brings in the most donated books will win a prize," she told them. "You can team up with another person if you want, but you must share the prize."

All of the students were excited about the book drive, but the Thompson twins were even more excited when they found out that the big prize was a new tent. Every summer the kids went camping in different areas, mostly while their parents did research for articles that they were writing. They enjoyed staying with their relatives and close friends of their parents, but they always missed their own friends. Although it was still two months away, they already had their first camping trip of the summer planned. They had permission to invite their friends along, and winning a new tent would come in handy.

After Mrs. Adams gave the class all of the details about the book drive, the class was let out. Stephanie and Steve met their best friends, Kamryn and Andrew, in front of the school.

"We could collect a lot of books with the four of us working together," Stephanie suggested.

"Who cares about books?" Andrew said. "I'm going to bike over to the old house after I get home. I want to find out if it's haunted."

"I'll try to meet you over there after dinner," Steve told his friend.

The twins rode the bus home from school since Tyler had baseball practice. Their mother greeted them at the door, and told them that it would be a while before dinner.

"We can make some phone calls while we are waiting for dinner and find out who might have books to donate," Stephanie said.

"Nah, I think I'll meet Andrew over at the haunted house," Steve said.

"Dinner won't be that late," their mother quickly told her son. "And that's enough cookies, you will both spoil your appetite."

As the twins ate their cookies; they discussed whom they might call for their book drive. Soon they had a list of ten people to call about donating books.

"We should call Mrs. Whipple first, before anyone else calls her. I bet she has some extra books," Stephanie said as she picked up the phone.

Stephanie soon found out that her guess was right about the retired English teacher having extra books. After she thanked her, Stephanie hung up and Steve called Mr. Jones, who owned a used book store before he retired. Steve found out that he also had some books that he could part with. As Steve was hanging up the phone, it rang, startling him and making him jump. Stephanie was laughing as she picked up the receiver.

"What's so funny?" Kamryn asked.

After Stephanie explained what had happened, Kamryn invited her and Steve over to the old house where a bunch of their friends were planning to meet. The teenagers wanted to see if the house was haunted. Stephanie quickly replied that they would be there and asked what time.

"Everyone is meeting at the old house about seven o'clock," Stephanie told her brother after she had hung up the phone.

"Cool. I just hope that we finish dinner by then so we can go," Steve said.

After the twins tried to call a few more people who were not home, Stephanie helped her mother with dinner and Steve set the table.

"Why are you two so energetic?" Tyler asked as he walked in the door and saw his brother and sister helping with dinner.

After the twins explained that they wanted to meet some friends at the new library site, Tyler smiled and volunteered to drive them.

"I have heard some strange things about that house also," he told them, "but I still don't believe it's haunted."

"We are just curious," Stephanie said.

It was almost seven o'clock by the time they had finished dinner and had left for the abandoned house. Reaching the house, the twins didn't think anyone was there, but then they saw Kamryn and Andrew standing by the side of the house. Andrew's older brother, Dylan, who was Tyler's best friend, was also there.

"Where is everyone?" Stephanie asked Kamryn.

"Apparently, most of the parents didn't want their kids hanging out around this house," she said with a sigh.

"So what do you think, Dylan?" sixteen-year-old Tyler asked. "Should we add this house to the list of haunted houses?"

"I haven't seen or heard anything strange yet," Dylan replied as they started to walk around the house.

The abandoned house was on top of Rampart Hill, overlooking Clear Creek Lake. It was easy to see how the lake got its name, with Colorado Blue Spruce trees reflected in the water. While Stephanie, who enjoyed writing, felt inspired to come back to the lake sometime to do some writing, the boys were thinking about fishing.

"Come on, guys, why are we just standing around?" Dylan asked. "We are here to check out the house."

From the outside the house looked huge. It was a two-story blue colonial that badly needed painting. The large wrap-around porch had round columns in the corners and on either side of the front stairs leading up to the porch. There were five large windows in the front and one big picture window.

The teenagers had often thought about going into the abandoned house, but they had never ventured inside.

"Should we try the door?" Steve asked his brother.

But before Tyler could even answer, they heard a loud, angry roar come from inside.

~

Chapter 2
The Threatening Stranger

"What was that?" Stephanie asked, her voice shaking.

"It sounded like a wild animal!" Steve answered.

Everyone agreed with Steve that it certainly didn't sound like a person, but none of them was really sure about an animal being in the house. They ran from the house and hid in some bushes to discuss what they had heard.

"That roar sounded loud and scary, but I don't think it could be real," Tyler commented. "I'll bet it is someone trying to scare us away."

"But why?" Stephanie asked.

"I don't know, but I would love to find out," her older brother replied.

Deciding that whoever was trying to scare them away could be dangerous, the teenagers left the house. Not much was said on the ride home except that everyone agreed not to tell anyone about the noise that they had heard. They didn't want to cause any unnecessary panic. They all agreed to meet at the house again the next night, right after school so they could further investigate the noise before dark.

The next day school seemed to last extra long for the twins as they anticipated going back to the old house that evening. Finally, the bell rang and they ran outside to meet their brother, who was waiting for them. They were leaving for the house when Stephanie remembered that they had already made plans to pick up books from Mrs. Whipple and Mr. Jones for the book drive.

"We'll just have to make a couple of stops," Tyler said.

The first stop was at the house of Mr. Jones, whom they had met through their parents. Mr. Jones fought in World War II and had helped their parents with an article they had written. He still walked with a limp from an old war wound and usually had a cane to help him get around. When they walked into his house, they found they were surrounded by books. The twins looked at the bookshelves with wide eyes.

"You could start a library right here," Stephanie said to Mr. Jones.

"Yeah, I know. Somehow I just couldn't part with all these books. I read them all the time." The black-haired man smiled. "But I did go through some of them, and I have four boxes for you."

After thanking Mr. Jones, the teens loaded the boxes in their dad's truck and headed for Mrs. Whipple's house. The elderly woman rarely had visitors and was glad to see them.

"Would you kids like some milk and cookies?" she asked. "I made them just for you."

The teenagers were anxious to get the books as quickly as possible and go to the old house. But they were polite and ate a few cookies as they told her about the new library.

"Right now the closest library we have is 20 miles away, and the new library will help a lot of us kids who live far out from Buena Vista. The new library is only a couple of miles from our house," Steve told her.

"It's good to hear that you kids are so excited about a new library," Mrs. Whipple said. "Good luck with the book drive."

After they had loaded the books into the truck and thanked Mrs. Whipple, they headed for the old house. They found their friends standing in front of the house next to a sign that read, "Future site of Rampart Library."

"Where have you guys been?" Dylan asked.

"We forgot about some books we were supposed to pick up," Tyler answered. "Was this sign here last night?"

"No, we were just talking about that," Dylan said. "They must have put this sign up sometime today."

"Don't you think the name Rampart Library is boring?" Kamryn said.

Rampart was a common name in the area. Rampart Hill, Rampart Reservoir, and Rampart Campground were just some of the names of the recreation spots nearby. They all agreed that the name was overused.

"I was thinking that it would be neat to name the library for the family who originally built the house," Stephanie said.

"That's a great idea," Kamryn agreed.

"Our teacher told us that the previous owners were named Smith, but she doesn't think that they are the ones who built the house," Stephanie said.

"Maybe we can find a clue to the original owners in the house," Steve said. "Speaking of the house, have you heard any noises yet?"

"We don't think anyone or anything is in there," Andrew replied.

"We looked in the windows and didn't see anything," Dylan added.

The teenagers checked all around the outside and took peeks in the windows again before they convinced themselves that it was safe to go inside. Tyler and Dylan were the first ones to walk up to the front door and slowly turn the knob, while the younger kids held their breath. After Tyler and Dylan checked inside the house, they called to the others that the house was vacant.

Inside they didn't see anything out of the ordinary. Tyler tried turning on a light in the living room, but the electricity was not working. Luckily, it was still light enough to see.

"What are we looking for, anyway?" Steve asked.

"Any kind of sound equipment, like a tape recorder or a microphone," Tyler answered.

"Don't forget to look for any clues that might lead us to the original owners of the house," Stephanie added.

But as they uncovered the furniture, they could see that there was not much to go on. A beat-up sofa, a rocking chair, and an old piano were the only furniture in the front room. Stephanie, who enjoyed playing the piano, fingered the keyboard.

"Boy, this is really out of tune," she said as she attempted to play the scales.

Upon entering the kitchen, they could see that it needed some work. The cabinets were unevenly stained and the flowered wallpaper was faded and peeling. A simple dining room table with six chairs was in the middle of the room, and an old hutch was along the right wall. They looked through all of the cupboards and the walk-in pantry, but they found everything empty.

The upstairs rooms were an even bigger disappointment to the teenagers. The first two bedrooms they walked into were completely empty.

"So far, it appears that the upstairs is empty," Steve commented.

"I think you're right," his friend, Andrew said. Andrew was a year younger than he was.

It was then that they heard a call from Stephanie, who had been in the next room, "Hey, come in here and look at this."

In another bedroom, toward the back of the house, Stephanie had uncovered a beautiful oak roll-top desk.

"I think it's Early American," Stephanie said as she looked inside the desk. Stephanie liked antiques.

"You mean it's an antique?" Steve asked.

"Oh yeah, I am sure of it," she answered.

"Is anything in it?" Tyler asked his sister.

"No, all of the drawers are empty," she replied as she opened each one.

"It doesn't make any sense that they would leave this beautiful desk behind," Steve thought aloud.

"Maybe they just forgot it," Andrew said.

"I wish we knew who left the desk," Stephanie said, "but it doesn't look like there are any clues in here."

They were about to leave the house when a thought came to Tyler.

"Wait, maybe there is a secret panel or other hidden area in the house," he said. "That sound we heard last night had to come from somewhere."

The teenagers checked the walls by pushing on the paneling to see if anything would open or slide, but found nothing. They also checked the floor for a trap door, but again came up with nothing.

Before leaving the property, they looked in the two-car detached garage that sat back from the house. They expected to find it as empty as the house and were surprised to find it full of equipment. Along the back wall was a pegboard full of hanging tools. In front of that was a long workbench with some old tools that were all rusted. There were also two lawn mowers, a small electric chain saw, and a couple of saw horses. In one corner of the garage there were brooms, rakes, shovels, a hose, and a couple of garbage pails.

"Why did they leave all this behind?" Steve asked.

"It's not worth much. Most of this stuff is all beat up, and I bet the lawn mowers and chain saw don't even work," Tyler said.

After going through everything in the garage, they still couldn't find anything that had the previous owner's name on it or any sound equipment that might have been used to scare them away last night.

"There is nothing here, let's go home," sixteen-year-old Dylan said.

Everyone agreed that it was getting late and decided to leave the house, but as the six friends were leaving, Steve suddenly stopped and pulled the others aside.

"Look over there in the woods. I think someone is watching us!" he whispered.

"Let's go see who it is," Steve said.

"No, I have a better idea. Let's act like we're leaving and then sneak back and see what the man does," Tyler suggested.

They got into their cars and drove away and then parked behind some bushes down the road. Then they walked back to where they could watch the house. At first nothing happened and then they saw a tall man with brown hair and glasses appear out of the woods. He walked up to the house and opened the front door and went inside.

"Let's go back and ask who he is," Stephanie said.

"Maybe he can tell us who built the house," Steve added.

They walked quietly back to the house and knocked on the front door. When no one answered, they peeked in the front picture window to see if they could tell what the man was doing, but he was nowhere in sight.

They tried knocking on the back door but again there was no answer. They looked through the kitchen window, but they still didn't see him.

"Let's knock on the front door again," Steve said. "We know that he is in there."

As they climbed the steps to the front porch, the stranger flung open the door and approached them before they reached the top step.

"What do you kids think you're doing?" he asked in an angry voice.

"We are just looking around," Stephanie bravely said. "Do you know who used to live in this house?"

"That's none of your business," he answered.

"They are going to turn it into a library." Steve started to explain why they were there, but the man wasn't listening.

"You kids better stay away from this house or you'll be sorry," he said as he went back inside the house, slamming the front door.

Tyler

Chapter 3
A Familiar Face

"Wow, he wasn't very friendly," Stephanie commented. "I bet he is the one that made that noise we heard."

"The question is why," Tyler said.

The teenagers said good-bye to each other and left in their two groups. As the Thompson kids rode home, they discussed why the man was so hostile. They figured that either he was homeless, or he was running from the law and either way they could tell he didn't want to be bothered. They decided that this time they should tell their parents about the strange man they had met.

After telling the story to their parents, they agreed to report the man to the police.

"He was trespassing as far as we know," Mr. Thompson said as he picked up the phone.

Since Tyler was the oldest, he told the police about the mysterious man. The police were very interested and said they would remind the city officials to change the locks now that the property had been sold.

After dinner, Stephanie called Kamryn and told her about their phone call to the police, but her friend had even better news.

"I just talked to Jamie, and her Mom knows the family that used to live in the house," Kamryn said. "She is going to ask her mom for their phone number and bring it to school tomorrow."

"That's great!" Stephanie said.

The next day, after school was let out, Stephanie and Kamryn found Jamie in front of the school.

"I got the address and phone number of the Smiths from my mother," Jamie told them.

"That's great, maybe the Smiths will know who originally built the house or at least who lived there before they did," Stephanie said.

Stephanie and Kamryn thanked their friend and it was decided that Stephanie would be the one to call the Smiths that night.

After Stephanie said good-bye to Kamryn, she found her brothers, who had agreed to help her collect more books after school. Since they had not had time to make phone calls, they hoped that they could find the people on their list home.

"Let's start at Mrs. Bentley's," Tyler said, "her house is the closest to here."

Mrs. Bentley, who had been Tyler's third-grade math teacher, was retired and lived alone in a small cottage near the center of town.

"I only have a few books," Mrs. Bentley told the Thompson kids, as she let them in her house, "but you're welcome to them. They have been sitting in my closet for a couple of years now."

"We can really use them," Stephanie assured her. "We need books on all kinds of subjects for the new library."

The Thompson kids stopped at the houses of a few more people on their list and although not everyone was home, they were still able to collect several boxes of books. They each were carrying a box of books when they walked into their house.

"I'm glad to see that you're excited about the possibility of winning a new tent, but I hope you're also excited about getting a new library so close to home," their father said.

"Oh, yeah, Dad. It will be great to be able to ride our bikes to the library," Stephanie said.

After dinner that night, Stephanie called the Smiths. When Mrs. Smith answered the phone, Stephanie briefly told her why she was calling.

"Yes, we lived in the house," Mrs. Smith said. "We bought the house through a real estate agent, but I'm afraid that I forget the previous owner's name."

Stephanie thanked the woman anyway and then went on to tell her about the library and the book drive.

"I have some books that I could donate," Mrs. Smith kindly told Stephanie. "Why don't you come by on Saturday?"

After writing down Mrs. Smith's address, Stephanie thanked her for her generosity and said they would see her on Saturday.

Tyler volunteered to drive Stephanie and Steve, who usually rode the bus, home from school the next day.

"I thought we could drive by the library and see if that man is still hanging around," he told them.

Driving by the Town Park, it was easy to tell that it was spring. People were out everywhere, walking their pets, playing catch, and riding bikes. They drove past Brown's Canyon, the part of the Arkansas River known as the white water capital of Colorado. People were lined up along the bank for their turn to go down the mighty river.

"Boy, that looks like fun," Tyler, who enjoyed white water rafting, commented.

But neither his brother nor his sister enjoyed rafting, and they didn't share their brother's enthusiasm. No one said anything as Tyler took a side road that was a shortcut to the library site. Tyler stopped when he saw that construction workers had already started work on the new library. They were painting the trim on the outside of the house and the columns around the porch. Other men were fixing the rain gutters along the roof and side of the house and hanging new shutters. A couple of men were cleaning the yard.

"Do you mind if we watch you work?" Tyler asked the men.

"Not as long as you stay out of the way. We have a lot of work to do," one of the men answered. "We could even put you to work if you want."

"Sure, that would be fun," Stephanie said. "We can't wait for the library to open."

"I wish my son were as enthusiastic about the library as you kids are, but he doesn't like reading much," another man commented.

"Oh, who is your son?" Steve asked.

When the man said that his name was Jimmy Holmes, Steve knew that he was talking about the red-haired kid who sat in the back of his history class. Jimmy didn't seem to like history that much either and drew pictures most of the time during class.

"I think he is in my history class," Steve said. "He keeps to himself mostly."

"Yeah, ever since his mother died, he has been in his own little world," the man said, frowning. "The therapist says that he just needs time, but it's been over a year."

Steve was ashamed of what he had thought about the boy he hardly knew. He asked God to forgive him and promised that he would go out of his way to be extra friendly toward the boy and then changed the subject.

"Where can we help?" Steve asked.

"Ask the men working inside," the first man who had spoken to them answered.

Inside the library, bookshelves were being put up along with partitions in different areas of what was once the living room. Where the bookcases were already in place, men had started to apply stain to them. The teenagers felt like they were just in the way of the workers so they decided to leave the house.

"I don't think there is much we can do right now," Stephanie said. "We'll be a bigger help after all the shelves are put in place."

"I wonder where that mysterious man is," Stephanie whispered to Tyler and Steve.

"It wouldn't surprise me if he were hiding somewhere, watching us," Steve answered.

"I don't care where he is," Tyler answered. "I'm taking both of you home and then I think I'll do some white water rafting."

On the drive home the twins told their brother about the field trip the class was to go on the next day.

"We are going to the Hall of Presidents Living Wax Studio in Colorado Springs tomorrow," Stephanie said.

"It's too bad you have already been there," Tyler said. "That will be boring for you."

"We don't care." Steve smiled. "We still get out of class."

"Don't forget the report we have to write," Stephanie reminded Steve, who frowned because he had forgotten that part.

The next day as they got on the bus for the field trip to Colorado Springs, Stephanie told Kamryn, about going by the library the night before.

"Was that man snooping around?" Kamryn asked.

"I don't think so, we didn't see him anywhere. Just a bunch of workers fixing up the place," Stephanie answered. "It is going to look nice when it's finished."

"I can't wait to see it," Kamryn agreed.

Meanwhile, Steve and Andrew were in line behind the girls to get on the bus. Steve nudged Andrew toward Jimmy, who was sitting by himself toward the back. Andrew didn't understand why Steve would want to sit with Jimmy, but he didn't have any objections. Jimmy didn't seem to mind either when Steve asked him if they could sit with him.

"OK, I guess," Jimmy answered, confused about why Steve was going out of his way to be nice to him.

"Isn't this a great way of getting out of school?" Steve asked, trying to break the ice.

"Looking at a bunch of wax figures isn't very interesting, but at least we don't have to sit in class," Andrew said.

Jimmy didn't comment but sat staring out the window. Steve decided to change the subject and started talking about the new library.

"Last night my brother, sister and I went by the new library. It's going to look nice when they are finished," he said. "Jimmy, the new library is a lot closer to where you live also, isn't it?"

"Yeah," Jimmy said, and then added, "I'm not much into books though."

"Me either," Andrew said. "I would rather be outside than stuck in a room somewhere."

"You can read outside too," Steve started to comment but didn't want to get into a debate so he asked Jimmy what he liked to do.

"Oh, I like watching television, going to the movies, and stuff like that," he said.

During the ride to Colorado Springs the three teenagers talked about their favorite movies and television shows. Steve invited Jimmy to come to the movies with them sometime, and Jimmy said he would have to see what he was doing. Although they didn't hit it right off, it was a step in the right direction, and Steve felt as if Jimmy really needed a friend right now.

When they reached the Wax Museum the three boys walked together for a while, but during one of the narratives, Jimmy wandered off by himself.

"What was all that about?" Andrew asked Steve.

"What do you mean?" Steve said.

"You know, your sudden interest in Jimmy," Andrew answered.

When Steve explained about talking with Jimmy's father at the library site, Andrew understood.

"That must be tough not to have a mother, and he seems like a nice kid," Andrew commented, and then changed the subject. "So which president are you doing your report on?"

"Oh, I already decided on Abraham Lincoln, that is, if no one gets him before me," Steve said.

"You better have a backup. Remember, Mrs. Adams is putting all of our names in a hat and then pulling them out one by one. You might be one of the last names she picks," Andrew said.

Later in the day, Steve found out that his friend was right. Abraham Lincoln had been picked long before his name was called. Andrew was lucky and got his choice of Theodore Roosevelt, Stephanie picked Ronald Reagan, and Kamryn selected Harry Truman. Finally, the teacher drew Steve's name, and he picked Calvin Coolidge from the list of presidents left.

On the ride home Andrew and Steve found seats together, and Jimmy actually asked if he could join them.

"Sure," Steve and Andrew said at once as they smiled at each other.

During the ride home, the three teenagers made plans to go to the movies together late Saturday afternoon. When Saturday finally arrived, the Thompson kids were up early to go the Smiths'. The family lived in the town of Salida, which was about half an hour from Buena Vista. When they reached the address that Mrs. Smith had given Stephanie over the phone, they saw that it was an apartment complex. They found number 65 and rang the bell.

Mrs. Smith came to the door and introduced herself as Silvia Smith and her husband as Jeremy. "When Jeremy lost his job, we just couldn't afford to live at the house anymore," she told the Thompson kids.

"That's too bad. Is the furniture left in the house yours?" Stephanie asked the woman.

"No, that furniture was left from the previous owners when we bought the house," she said. "I didn't bring it in the move because it reminded me of that house."

When Stephanie asked her about the roll-top desk, the woman looked sad.

"That was a favorite of mine. I used to sit at the desk and write letters to all my relatives," she told them. "My husband and I got into an argument because he wanted to bring it to this house but having the desk here would have been too depressing for me."

As Mrs. Smith mentioned the argument that she had with her husband, Jeremy got up and left the room. But it didn't seem to bother Mrs. Smith.

"I'm glad to see that there will be some good to come out of all of this. The real estate agent that sold the house to us was a Carol Bennett. Maybe she can help you locate the original owners," she said.

Mrs. Smith gave the teenagers the books she had promised to donate, and the teens started to leave after thanking the woman. But as they were walking out the door, Stephanie suddenly stopped in her tracks. Hanging on the wall next to the front door were several pictures.

Stephanie pointed to one of the pictures and asked Mrs. Smith, "Who is the boy in this picture?"

"Oh, that is my son," she said. "Isn't he handsome?"

"Oh, yes," Stephanie agreed.

Outside the house Stephanie whispered to her brothers. "Did you see that? The man in that picture looks like the man that we saw at the old house!"

Stephanie

Chapter 4
A Find from the Past

Stephanie's brothers agreed that the picture at Mrs. Smith's house did look like the man who they had seen at the old house.

"But the man that yelled at us was a lot older than the boy in the picture," Steve said.

"It could still be the same person," Tyler said.

"Should we say something to Mrs. Smith?" Stephanie asked her brothers.

"I don't think so," Tyler said. "Not yet, anyway, let's wait and see if we can find out more on our own."

"I think you're right," Steve agreed. "But now I really want to find out what is going on with that house."

When they got home from their drive to Salida, Steve biked over to Andrew's house, where he found Andrew and Jimmy playing a game of catch in the backyard.

"I'm glad that you're here," Andrew said when he saw Steve. "My mom can drive us to the movies, if we leave right now."

On the way, Steve told Andrew about seeing the picture that looked just like the man they had seen at the library.

"Wow! Then that man must have lived in that house at some time, since his parents lived there," Andrew said.

"What man are you talking about?" Jimmy inquired.

As they continued toward the movie theater, Steve began filling Jimmy in on the mysterious man at the old house

Meanwhile, back at the Thompson house, Stephanie tried calling Carol Bennett, the real estate agent that Mrs. Smith had mentioned to the kids. Unfortunately, Ms. Bennett was on vacation for the rest of the week the secretary told her.

After thanking her, Stephanie hung up the phone and got ready to leave for Kamryn's house. The girls had made plans to do research for their president reports. It would be the last reports before the end of the school year so they wanted to get them finished as soon as possible. Stephanie enjoyed writing and thought that Ronald Reagan was an interesting president. Kamryn, on the other hand, wasn't very excited about writing her report on Harry Truman but knew she had to do a good job because she wanted to bring her history grade up.

Stephanie couldn't wait to tell Kamryn about the picture they had seen at Mrs. Smith's house. She was glad that it was only a short bike ride to her house.

"Maybe it's just someone who resembles the man we saw," Kamryn said.

"That could be, but it doesn't seem likely," Stephanie said. "If the man is Mrs. Smith's son, then he lived in the house at some point, and if he was in trouble, the house would be a logical hiding place."

Kamryn agreed with her friend as they started to work on their reports. They had worked on the reports for a couple of hours when Kamryn's mother invited Stephanie to stay for dinner. After Stephanie called home and got her parents permission, she accepted the invitation. Stephanie enjoyed having dinner at Kamryn's, because her mom was such a good cook. After a big pot roast dinner, Stephanie and Kamryn played a game of crazy eights before it was time for Stephanie to go home.

The next day was Sunday and the Thompson family spent it together. After church services, they enjoyed a drive through the mountains. Stephanie was talking about her report on Ronald Reagan when Steve suddenly asked his dad to stop the car.

"Look," he said, pointing to a herd of elk.

When the car stopped, Steve jumped out with his camera. His father was close behind with the tripod. They were able to get several pictures before the elk ran off.

The family continued down the road and soon found the perfect picnic spot. It wasn't long before they were all full of fried chicken, potato salad, and coleslaw. After they ate, the teenagers played catch before the family headed home.

On Monday, Tyler went to the Town Hall where he looked up the address of the old house to see if there were any records of who built it.

"That's the house that the city just bought in a foreclosure sale," the clerk said, trying to be helpful.

"Yeah, our school is working with the city to turn it into a library for us kids who live far out in the foothills," he told the clerk. "We are hoping to find out who built the house so we can name the library after them. We already talked to the people who lost the house, Jeremy and Silvia Smith, but they couldn't remember the name of the people who lived there before them."

"Let's see what we can find out," the clerk said as she looked up the address. "The records show that Jeremy and Silvia Smith did live in the house, but I'm afraid that it doesn't go back any further than that. The records of the previous owners must have gotten lost when Buena Vista got its own Town Hall."

Tyler met Stephanie and Steve at their usual meeting spot after school.

"Well, I didn't find out anything when I went to the Town Hall," he told them.

"Oh, well, something is bound to turn up," Stephanie said.

"Yeah, meanwhile, let's win that book drive," Steve said. "I thought of a couple more places to check for donated books."

The three teenagers all agreed that it was a good idea and headed for Mrs. Bradley's house. She was Steve's English teacher from last year.

"I heard about this book drive," she said smiling. "It's good to see that you kids are so involved."

"We really enjoy reading, and it will be nice to have a library so close to home," Stephanie said.

"I just wish I had some books to give you," the woman sighed. "Perhaps if I look in the attic..."

"Oh, we don't want you to go to any trouble," Tyler spoke up.

"I'll tell you what, my son is coming over here tomorrow night, I will have him help me look for some books. If I find any books, I'll give you a call," she said.

"That will be fine," Stephanie replied, smiling.

The next person that Steve thought of was Mr. Constance who was a professor at Buena Vista Community College. The short, stocky man was very helpful and contributed a couple of boxes of books.

"Good luck with the book drive, and I hope these books will help," he said as he waved good-bye.

"More books!" their mother exclaimed when all three of them walked in the door each carrying a box of books. "At the rate you kids are going, you're sure to win the tent."

"Yeah, we certainly have a lot of books to go through," Stephanie told her mother and then asked her mother what she was baking.

"These are desserts for the charity fund-raiser that I volunteered for," she said. "It's tomorrow afternoon and I'm afraid that I forgot all about it. You kids will have to fix dinner for yourselves tonight."

"Is it all right if we order pizza?" Stephanie asked her mother. "The teacher wants only books that are in good condition, and we want to go through as many boxes as we can tonight."

Their mother agreed that pizza was fine with her and the teens started going through the boxes after the pizza was ordered. They had three boxes sorted by the time Tyler left to go get the pizza. Tyler carried the boxes out to the car and then drove to the pizza parlor.

Buena Vista, being a small town, had only one pizza parlor, located in the center of town. It was a good drive just to get pizza, unlike where they had lived in Westminster, where they could walk to get pizza. Still Tyler didn't mind the drive at all on this nice spring evening. He drove past one of his favorite fishing spots along Cottonwood Creek, where he saw Dylan trying to catch some trout.

"Hey, how's the fishing?" he asked his friend.

"Nothing so far," Dylan answered. "Want to join me?"

"Sorry, I can't, I'm going to pick up some pizza and then I promised Stephanie and Steve that I would help them sort books," Tyler said.

"Hey, could you bring back a couple of slices for me?" Dylan asked with a big smile on his face. "I promised myself that I wouldn't leave until I caught some fish and that looks like it could be a long while."

Tyler promised his friend that he would stop back on the way home and headed for the pizza parlor. As Tyler entered the restaurant, he saw a familiar face sitting at the counter.

"Hi," he said to the man.

When the man didn't respond, Tyler figured that the man must not have heard him.

"Hi, aren't you the guy that . . . " Tyler wasn't even able to finish his sentence before the man just turned around and walked out of the pizza parlor.

"Hey, where did your friend go?" The clerk at the counter asked Tyler.

"I don't know but I'll be right back," Tyler said, and quickly walked outside to see where the man had gone.

When he couldn't see which direction the man had gone, Tyler shrugged his shoulders and then turned to walk back into the pizza parlor.

"Hey, watch it, kid," a tall, dark-haired man said bumping into Tyler.

"Sorry," Tyler mumbled.

Tyler wondered where the man had come from as he followed him into the pizza parlor.

"So did you find your friend?" the person at the register immediately asked Tyler.

"I don't even know him," Tyler explained. "I just said hello to him."

"He left his pizza," the man said grimly.

On the way home, Tyler stopped to give Dylan some pizza as he had promised. He told him what had happened at the restaurant.

"All you said was 'hi'?" Dylan asked.

"That's all, strange, huh?" Tyler said. "Enjoy the pizza and good luck catching some fish."

When Tyler reached the house, he ran inside. His mother was taking pies out of the oven.

"Hey, no running. I almost dropped this pie," she said. "What's the big hurry?"

Stephanie and Steve heard their brother come in and joined their mother in the kitchen. Tyler filled them all in on the incident at the pizza parlor.

"Guess who I saw at the pizza parlor?" he directed his question to Stephanie and Steve.

"Who?" they asked in unison.

"The guy who was at the old house!" he said. "I said 'hi' to him, and he just walked away without his pizza."

"He isn't very friendly," Steve commented.

"It's not a crime to be unfriendly," Stephanie said and then added, "but it sure is strange that he didn't even want to acknowledge you."

Normally, the teenagers were not allowed to eat in the family room but their mother made an exception this time so they could go through the books as they ate. Tyler helped the twins sort books because he also wanted to win the tent. The three teenagers had been sorting books for only a few minutes when Steve found one about Leadville, Colorado, that interested him.

"Steve, could you help us sort books. You can read that book later," Stephanie said.

"This book is very interesting" Steve said. "It tells a story about three Irish brothers who quit their jobs hoping that they might hit silver at a place called Strayhorse Gulch. They started digging a prospect hole but ran out of money so they sent one of the brothers back to work. That night the two brothers came back to find the other brother and tell him the news that they found a rich vein. They named their mine the Camp Bird and then they went on to strike the Charleston and Pine mines."

"That's very interesting, but could you read about it later?" Stephanie asked again.

Not long after Stephanie said this, she became absorbed in her own book. There was no picture on the cover or even a title. The book was covered with a green velvet piece of cloth and was written by hand. She opened the book and started reading.

It is quickly getting colder. Winter will soon be upon us as the days become shorter and the nights longer. Many miners, who had little to begin with, are now becoming desperate for food and clothing to keep them warm. Others have money to burn (or so it seems) as they go from one dance hall to another till they are in drunken slumber.

I am so lucky to have a man like Charlie who doesn't enjoy the saloons and loud casinos for he is a hardworking man who takes great pride in himself and his family.

Of course, he did have hopes of striking it rich just like the others. But after working the California Gulch many long hours just to find black sand clogging the sluice boxes, he has gone back to his known trade as a blacksmith. With the money he has made, we have been fortunate to leave our tent and pay for a nice cabin here in Oro City. They have coined this place Gold City but what good is it to have gold in an area if it can't be mined?

As Stephanie read the book that she had found, Tyler had started reading a book about his favorite baseball team, the Colorado Rockies, and now Steve was getting annoyed.

"Come on, guys, are you going to help or what? You got upset when I was reading," he said.

Tyler put his book down and continued sorting books, but Stephanie found her book so interesting that she couldn't put it down. She continued reading.

Blacksmithing has surely paid off for Charlie but it has been rumored that silver has been discovered on Iron and Carbonate Hills. I'll never forget that look in Charlie's eyes when he told me this; they were so full of wonder and hope. So although it makes me a little uneasy, I told Charlie that I would support his decision to get in on a claim with a couple of other men before it's too late. It will not be easy for the men, as they must work very quickly. Once a miner has driven his stakes, he is only given sixty days to start a shaft or the claim can legally be jumped. Of course, there are many men who don't worry about the law at all so the men must also guard the claim night and day. I have to end this for now as it is getting awful late but I have to admit that I too am hopeful of finding silver.

"Hey, if you think that the books you found are interesting, look what I found," Stephanie exclaimed. "It's an old journal!"

Chapter 5
The Warning

"Does it say who it belongs to?" Tyler asked her.

"No, I don't see anyone's name on it," Stephanie said.

"Let me see that," Stephanie's mother said, coming over to them.

"Isn't the velvet cover beautiful?" Stephanie said. "I wonder who it belongs to."

"Well, I don't know to whom it belongs, but I think you should try to find out before you just start reading it," her mother said.

"But there is no name," Stephanie said.

"You should check with everyone who donated books and ask them if they have ever seen this book," her mother replied.

Stephanie agreed, knowing that her mother was right. She was too tired by then to read the journal anyway so she put it with her schoolbooks.

After school the next day, Stephanie met Kamryn in the hall.

"Do you want to come over to my house?" her friend asked.

"Sorry, I can't. I found a mysterious journal and I want to find out who it belongs to" Stephanie said.

"How exciting," Kamryn said. "Good luck, let me know what you find out."

Stephanie found her brothers, who were talking with Dylan and Andrew.

"Come on, we have to get to the places we went to yesterday," she said.

"We can do that anytime," Steve said irritated.

"What is she talking about?" Andrew said.

The brothers told their friends about the journal she had found.

"What's the big deal about a journal anyway?" Andrew asked.

"Maybe there's a secret in it," Stephanie said.

"Steve, how about if I drop you off at home to sort through the books we collected, and I can drive Stephanie back to where we were yesterday," Tyler suggested.

"Yeah, I guess that would be all right," Steve agreed.

"I don't understand why you're so interested in books," Andrew, who didn't like to read, said to Steve before they said good-bye.

Steve, however, enjoyed reading and looked forward to going through the books. So Tyler dropped him off, and he and Stephanie went to see Mr. Jones, who was not much help.

"With all the books I have, I couldn't tell you if it came from here or not. It's a good possibility that it got mixed in with some books that I bought from someone else," he said.

"Maybe we'll have better luck at Mrs. Whipple's or Mrs. Bentley's," Tyler said, trying to cheer his sister up.

Unfortunately, after visiting Mrs. Whipple and Mrs. Bentley, the teenagers learned that they weren't much help either. Mrs. Whipple didn't remember a journal but said her memory wasn't very good anymore and Mrs. Bentley said that it may have come from her grandmother's estate but she didn't recognize it.

"It is getting dark, and we've been everywhere, so we might as well head home," Stephanie said, disappointed.

On the way home, Tyler drove past the library site.

"Look, there's a light on in the house," Stephanie said pointing to the house. "None of the workers should be in the house this late."

"No, and it appears that the light is coming from a candle," Tyler said. "The light looks like it is flickering."

"Let's go closer and see if we can see who is in the house," Tyler suggested.

"Yeah, maybe it's the man we saw before," Stephanie said.

The teenagers prowled around to the back of the house where it was less likely that they would be

noticed. Peeking in the back window, they soon saw that their guess was right. A candle sat on the kitchen table and the brown haired man was using a flashlight to look through the empty cupboards in the kitchen.

"What could he be looking for?" Stephanie asked her brother.

"I don't know but it must be something really important for him to search so thoroughly," her brother answered.

As the man continued his search, the Thompson kids tried to get a better look. Suddenly, they heard a noise coming from the woods behind them. The man must have heard the noise too, because he shone his flashlight out the window toward the woods. Tyler and Stephanie quickly ducked below the window so they wouldn't be seen.

"Come on," Tyler whispered, after the flashlight was no longer shining out the window.

They jumped into the car, but did not see anyone come after them.

"Do you think he saw us?" Stephanie asked as they drove away.

"I don't know but I'm pretty sure I saw someone watching us from the woods," Tyler said.

"Why would someone be watching us?" Stephanie asked.

"Maybe they are hiding out in the house also," Tyler said. "This is turning out to be much more than just naming a library."

When Tyler and Stephanie arrived home, they told Steve about the events that had taken place at the old house.

"I wish I had decided to go with you," Steve said.

Before dinner was ready the teenagers discussed the various reasons why the man might be snooping around the old house.

"Maybe he knows there is something valuable hidden," Stephanie said.

"Or maybe he is trying to find something that he doesn't want anyone else to find before the new library opens," Tyler said.

It was certainly a puzzle and the teenagers were excited about solving the mystery. Even though they couldn't do anything about him that night, the mysterious man was still on everyone's mind.

After dinner that night Steve went into Stephanie's bedroom to see what she was doing.

"I'm reading the journal that I found," she told him.

"I thought Mom didn't want you to read it before you found the owner." Steve said.

"I got her to change her mind," Stephanie told her brother. "After all, it was donated to the library, and we may never find its owner."

Steve still didn't understand her interest in the journal and left her room and went to find his brother, who wasn't home.

"He went over to Dylan's house to shoot hoops,"

Steve's mother told him. "You can help me do the dishes."

"I'm just bored, not desperate," he said, and then added, "I think I will go read my book about silver mines in Leadville."

Meanwhile, Stephanie went on to read the journal.

After many long months of waiting, the effort that the men have put into working their claim, has finally paid off. They have named their shaft the Silver Spoon after the silver they found. The first luxury item that Charlie bought for me was this beautiful roll-top desk made of solid oak. I saw one like it at the doctor's office and I told Charlie how beautiful it was. At the time, I had just given up the writing table in exchange for food, depriving my mother of my weekly letters. My new desk was handcrafted by well-known furniture maker, Gregory Hamilton, who has carefully placed each piece of wood so that the corners fit perfectly. The carved wood and the great detail that has been put into the desk are meticulous. The pigeonholes in the desk are conveniently arranged to hold assorted items such as mail. A wooden curtain can be pulled down and locked to keep the dust or unwanted people out of the desk. It is clear that the artist took his time in designing the desk. I feel so lucky to have a husband who not only loves me, but he also wants me to have the finest things. Now, I will write letters to my mother and all of my close friends on my new desk. I hope some of them will come to Colorado with their families to prosper. We are not the only ones to strike silver, many families have made some big hits.

Stephanie could just imagine the woman sitting at her beautiful roll-top desk writing. As she was picturing her, suddenly her eyes lit up and she jumped up and ran to find her brothers. Steve was lying on his bed reading when she entered his room.

"I just thought of something," Stephanie said. "In the journal the woman tells about a special roll-top desk that her husband Charlie bought for her," she said.

"So what?" Steve shrugged his shoulders.

"Don't you see? The desk mentioned in the journal sounds just like the roll-top desk at the old house," Stephanie said.

As Stephanie told her brother about her theory on the desk, she suddenly realized that they had forgotten to check with Mrs. Smith about the journal.

"It seems like just a coincidence," he said, frowning. "There are a lot of roll-top desks around."

However, when Tyler arrived home he though that Stephanie could be on to something.

"You don't find too many roll-top desks just sitting around abandoned houses," he said. "Besides, it makes sense, if the journal came from the Smiths, it could have been left at the old house just like the desk was."

"Well, then, why don't you just call Mrs. Smith and ask her about it?" Steve asked his twin.

Since it was too late that night to call Mrs. Smith, Stephanie planned to call her the next day when she got home. However, she forgot all about calling her when she picked up the mail the next day after school. In the mail there was a letter addressed to the Thompson kids. Stephanie opened the envelope and gasped at the typed note inside:

Stay away from Rampart Hill or else!

Steve

Chapter 6
A Possible Clue

"What's wrong, Stephanie?" Steve asked when he saw the concerned look on his sister's face.

"Listen to this note that we got in the mail," she said. "It says in bold type, 'Stay away from Rampart Hill or else!'"

"Or else what?" Tyler laughed.

"Well, I don't think this note is one bit funny," their mother said. "It's a good thing the library is opening in a week. Meanwhile, I don't want you kids near that place unless you are with an adult."

"Stephanie, let's not worry about the note," Tyler said. "Why don't you call Mrs. Smith and ask her if the journal could have come from her donated books?"

Stephanie took her brother's advice and phoned Mrs. Smith's right away. After she hung up with her, she gave her brothers the good news.

"She recognized the description of the journal!" Stephanie exclaimed to her brothers. "She said that it had been left there by the previous owners. She actually found it in the desk but she said that she had only read a few pages and had never finished it."

"Okay, so I guess you were right," Steve said.

"But that's not everything. She also told me that her son, Chip, was visiting a few months ago, and she thinks he might have read the journal."

"I'll bet the mysterious man at the old house is Chip Smith and he knows about something mentioned in that journal," Tyler suggested. "Stephanie, you need to finish that book."

"We need to find out who lived in the house before the Smiths," Stephanie said.

"Wait a minute, what about the real estate agent?" Steve asked. "Shouldn't she be back from vacation by now?"

"That's right, I'll give her a call" Stephanie said, picking up the phone.

Carol Bennett wasn't in but Stephanie was able to talk with her assistant, Linda. She explained briefly about naming the library and trying to find out the original owners' names.

"Yes, that sounds good," Stephanie said after listening into the phone for a short period. "Thanks for your help."

"Well?" her twin brother asked immediately.

"I talked to her assistant, who said that she has a hectic schedule," Stephanie explained. "She suggested that we stop by the office in a couple of days."

"I hope she can help us. It won't be long until the dedication ceremonies," Steve said.

At school the next day, Mrs. Adams reminded the class about their president reports due at the end of the week.

"Also, I hope you all remembered that tomorrow night after school we will be going over to help clean up the new library," she said. "I am trusting that all of you have rides lined up, and you're to let me know right away if there are any problems."

The twins looked at each other across the classroom. In all of the excitement, they had forgotten all about their commitment to help clean the library.

During lunch Stephanie and Steve joined Kamryn and Andrew at their table. Stephanie filled their friends in on their idea of going to see the real estate agent who had sold the old house.

"We were going to go over there tomorrow night, but we forgot all about the cleanup," Stephanie said.

"Maybe we'll find a clue at the house while we are cleaning," Andrew suggested.

The teenagers brightened at the idea. Andrew was right. There could be a clue just hidden by some dust or dirt that they overlooked when they searched the house before.

That night after school Stephanie and Kamryn got together to finish their president reports.

"I think you should expand on his time being an actor," Kamryn told Stephanie, referring to President Reagan.

"But he wasn't a president then," Stephanie reasoned.

Kamryn found another section, which Stephanie did agree to expand. They had a pattern down for getting their reports written and it worked well for them. It did not take long to finish their reports and then they had time to go roller-blading.

Meanwhile, Steve and Andrew were at the Thompson house just getting started on their reports.

"I don't know why I had to get Calvin Coolidge, anyway," Steve was complaining. "There isn't too much about him on this encyclopedia CD."

"Hey, wait, you just skipped past Theodore Roosevelt," Andrew told Steve.

Steve backed up to where Theodore Roosevelt's name appeared and double-clicked the mouse for more information.

"Don't you have enough information?" Steve asked.

"There is so much about Roosevelt that I want to get the right facts," Andrew said. "This will be our last major history grade, you know."

"Don't remind me, I only have a C in history" Steve frowned. "I have to get a good grade on this report."

Andrew promised Steve that after he was finished rewriting the notes he had taken, he would help Steve find more information on Coolidge. But the night just seemed to fly by and Steve didn't find any more information.

"I'll try to look him up on my dad's computer and print out anything I can find," Andrew told Steve as he said good-bye.

The next night after school was the big cleanup. As the teenagers helped clean, they were still looking for clues to what had made that awful noise the first night they had come by the house. As the night progressed, they were losing hope.

Since it had been decided to leave what little furniture had been left in the house for the library's use, the furniture needed cleaning up. While several students dusted and polished the furniture, others swept the floors and washed the windows. The kitchen, which was going to be used only for special occasions, was cleaned with disinfectant.

After they were done with their part of the cleaning, Stephanie and Kamryn went upstairs to the desk, which fascinated both of them.

"I wonder if there is a secret compartment somewhere," Stephanie said, as she looked the desk over. She found a small drawer underneath but could find nothing else in the desk.

"I described the desk to my mother, who said that the desk is probably about a hundred and twenty years old," Kamryn was saying to Stephanie when Steve called them downstairs.

"Look what Jimmy found," he said, showing them a tape recorder.

"Where did you find it?" Stephanie asked.

"I had to go down to the basement to get some boxes. It was hidden under one of them, next to the window," Jimmy said.

"So that's where that scary noise came from," Kamryn said.

Andrew pushed the "play" button on the recorder and quickly turned the volume down as the roar that they had heard the first night echoed through the basement.

"We still need to figure out who put it there," Steve, said as he turned it off.

"Maybe there are fingerprints on it," Jimmy suggested.

"Yeah, we can take it to the police station to be analyzed," Steve said. "The only problem is that we have all touched it."

The teenagers were discouraged until they remembered the tape that was in the recorder. They had played the tape but no one had actually touched it. On the way home they stopped by the police station to have the tape checked for fingerprints.

"We can check the tape for fingerprints, but it will take some time to try and match them," one of the officers said after they told him their story.

The following day they went to Home Realty where they met Carol Bennett.

"What can I do for you?" she said as she introduced herself.

"About eight years ago you sold a house up on Rampart Hill to a Jeremy and Silvia Smith," Stephanie said. "We are trying to find out who owned the house before them."

"Eight years ago, now let me think," she said. "That was awhile ago. I don't think that I could remember."

"The house is a blue colonial with a large wrap-around porch," Stephanie said.

After the agent had gone through her file cabinet for several minutes, she came back over to the teenagers.

"I'm afraid that I don't have any records going that far back here in the office. I would have to go through the records that I have stored at my home" she said. "Why do you want to know who owned the house?"

Stephanie told her about the new library and their idea of naming it after the people who originally built the house.

"That is a great idea," she said. "I would be happy to check through my old records and give you a call if I find anything."

After Stephanie gave Carol their phone number, they thanked the agent and headed for home. On the way home they stopped by the police station to see if the fingerprints on the tape had been analyzed.

"We checked the fingerprints from the tape on our computerized file of criminal fingerprints, but none of them matched up," the officer told them.

"What do we do now?" Tyler asked the officer. "Someone planted that tape recorder to scare us. Who knows what they might do next time."

"It was probably just a prank, by one of your friends," the officer said. "We'll keep the tape recorder for evidence. Let us know if anything else happens that seems suspicious."

That night after dinner, Steve suggested that they play a game of Monopoly.

"Don't you have to work on your report?" Stephanie asked her brother.

"I don't feel much like working on it right now," Steve said. "I still have time."

"If you think two days is enough time," Stephanie commented as they got the Monopoly board out.

It wasn't long before Tyler owned most of the properties including Boardwalk and Park Place, which he had already started putting houses on. Stephanie owned Illinois, Indiana, and Kentucky Avenues while Steve owned Pennsylvania, North Carolina, and Pacific Avenues. The rest of the properties were divided among the three of them, with each owning one railroad.

As Steve landed on the B. & O. Railroad, which was the last one to be purchased, he said, "I'll buy that."

It was then Stephanie's turn and she landed on Boardwalk.

"That will be $200," Tyler said.

Tyler was obviously winning. Both Steve and Stephanie owned property but were not able to put houses up as quickly as Tyler. The twins hung in there for over an hour but Stephanie had to mortgage some of her properties and Steve was even worse off.

"I'm bankrupt," he said. "I give up. You win, Tyler."

Tyler turned to Stephanie, "What about you?"

"I'm out too. Anyway, I want to read some more of the journal," she said.

After they put away their game, Tyler went to his room to watch a movie while Steve decided that he should work on his report. He just wished he had more information. Even Andrew had looked up President Coolidge on the Internet but had not found much. Maybe there was more information on one of their books in the home library that his parents had put together, Steve thought as he walked down the hall. In the library, he found his mother writing and told her his problem.

"You might find something at the Colorado Springs Library," she said.

But when Steve told her that the report was due in only two days, she couldn't believe it.

"If you don't find anything, it's your own fault for waiting until the last minute," she said frowning. "You might try looking in some of our history books."

After Steve opened the first history book, he started feeling relieved. For some reason there was more information in this book than he had found on the computer.

As he was writing notes, Stephanie was in her room reading more of the journal. She wished she knew who wrote the journal. The author sounded so nice, and it was clear that she loved Charlie.

> *I am sitting at the beautiful roll-top desk that Charlie so thoughtfully bought for me. He continues to buy me nice things, beautiful dresses, store-bought dishes, and jewelry. I have put all my treasures in the beautiful trunk that he bought for me and have hidden the key. I look forward to the day when we will be able to share that love with our children.*

Stephanie's cat jumped up on her bed looking for attention. She played with Lucky for a few minutes before continuing to read.

> *I have great news for I have just come from the doctors to find out that I am with child. Now that the silver market has dwindled, I am unsure of when and how I should tell Charlie my news. I know he has often wished he had a son even though he has tried hard not to let on. He assures me that the silver market will hit again and then we will be showered with wealth.*

Stephanie couldn't believe what she was reading. It sounded so romantic and it left her with so many questions. How bad was the silver market? Would Charlie just go back to blacksmithing when he found out about the baby? Why didn't she want to tell him she was pregnant? As she was thinking this, the phone rang, interrupting her thoughts.

"Stephanie, it's for you," her mother called.

Stephanie was surprised to find out that the call was from Carol Bennett, the real estate agent that they had talked to a few days ago.

"I apologize for calling so late but I found the names of the owners for you," the real estate agent told her.

"That's great!" Stephanie said. "What were their names?"

"Charlie and Debbie Essex," she answered.

"Could it be the same Charlie who was in the journal?" Stephanie wondered.

Dylan

Chapter 7
A Great Surprise

"Hello, Stephanie, are you still there?" The real estate agent asked when Stephanie didn't say anything.

"Oh, yes, I am," Stephanie said. "Sorry, I was just thinking about something. Thank you so much for looking up the information for us. You have been a big help."

It wasn't until after Stephanie hung up that she realized that it couldn't be the same Charlie who was in the journal because it had been written sometime around the late 1800's. Still, she was excited about getting the names of the people who had once lived in the house. She found her brothers to tell them the news.

"That was the real estate agent on the phone. She gave me the names of the people who lived in the house, Charlie and Debbie Essex. I hope they are still at the same address that the real estate agent gave me. The address she had in the file for them is in Salida," Stephanie said.

"That's good news," Mrs. Thompson said as she walked in the living room. "Tomorrow you can try calling them but for now it's time for bed."

Stephanie looked forward to calling Mr. and Mrs.

Essex and dialed information when she got home from school the next day. After getting their number, she crossed her fingers and dialed. She was delighted to find that it was the right number when Mrs. Essex answered. Stephanie explained briefly about the library going in the house on Rampart Hill.

"Oh, yes, we did live there," Debbie said. "We would love to hear more about this library, can you come by our condo on Saturday?"

"That would be perfect," Stephanie replied. "I look forward to meeting you."

After Stephanie hung up the phone, she went to tell her brothers the good news.

"Tyler and Steve are not here," Mrs. Thompson reminded her. "They have baseball practice."

"Oh yeah, I forgot," Stephanie said and then told her mother the good news.

But when Stephanie asked her mother if she could drive them to the Essex's house, her mother informed her of a neighborhood board meeting that she already had planned to attend.

Stephanie hoped her brother could drive them, as she couldn't wait to meet Charlie and Debbie Essex. She called Kamryn to tell her the news.

When Stephanie told her that she had found out who lived in the house, Kamryn wanted to hear all about it.

"Hold on," she told Stephanie. A few minutes later Kamryn came back to the phone and said that her mom could drive her over to Stephanie's house.

When Kamryn arrived, Stephanie told her about the conversation with Mrs. Essex.

"Hopefully, we can go meet her on Saturday," she said.

"That's exciting," Kamryn said. "Do you think it would be okay if I come along too?"

"I don't see why not, that is, if Tyler can drive us," Stephanie said.

While Stephanie and Kamryn were waiting for Tyler and Steve to come home to tell them the news, they listened to a new CD that Kamryn had brought. They did each other's hair while they listened.

"I was starting to think that we would never find out who lived in that house," Stephanie said.

"Do you still think Mrs. Essex is the one who wrote the journal?" Kamryn asked.

"It really doesn't give us many clues," Stephanie told her friend. "But I don't think so, whoever wrote it would be well over a hundred years old by now."

"Why don't we read some of it now?" Kamryn said, and then added, "I'm interested in it as much as you are."

Stephanie turned to the bookmark she had placed in the journal and started to read.

Charlie has finally given up mining for the time being and has opened his own blacksmith shop but business is slow. Many people have left Oro City, and it feels so deserted. It's like we are in the middle of nowhere. Charlie must travel to find customers, so he is gone a lot. Charlie wishes that he could be home to help more, but it's impossible because of his long hours. It is not an easy task to raise two children all by myself.

"Children?" Stephanie stopped to exclaim. "She must have stopped writing in the journal for a while. The last thing I had read was that she was pregnant."

James and Augusta are such handfuls. They are at that age where they are dealing with sibling rivalry and are constantly fighting. Charlie tells of a rumor of gold somewhere in the high country. He is looking into it to see if there is any truth to the rumor. I can only dream that it is true, as it would be nice to live in luxury but even if it isn't true, I am truly thankful for what we have. It is much more than most people who lost everything because of their greed.

"So they lived in Leadville where they had found silver but the silver market dropped so Charlie had to go back to being a blacksmith," Kamryn said.

"That's what it sounds like." Stephanie agreed.

Soon Tyler and Steve came home from baseball practice.

"Hey, guys, come in here for a minute," Stephanie called from her room.

"This had better be good, Steph. We are both ready for a shower," Tyler said.

"Yeah, and I have to finish that dumb report that is due tomorrow," Steve said.

When Stephanie told them about her phone call to Mrs. Essex, they were both as thrilled as Stephanie.

"Yeah, I guess I can make time to drive you kids over there on Saturday," Tyler said in a teasing voice.

"Oh, thank you, Sir," Stephanie teased back. "We do know how busy your social schedule is these days."

When Saturday finally arrived, the Thompson kids picked up Kamryn and then headed for Charlie and Debbie Essex's house. They lived in a large con-dominium development with a southwestern décor. It was a beautiful spring day and many people were out on the balconies or patios. They found number 1403, which Mrs. Essex had given Stephanie over the phone.

When the front door opened, a very friendly woman who looked to be in her seventies greeted them.

"You must be the Thompson kids," she said smiling.

"All but one of us. I am Stephanie and these are my brothers, Tyler and Steve, and this is my best friend, Kamryn." Stephanie said, introducing everyone.

The woman welcomed them in and said to call her Deb. She introduced her husband, Charlie, who was sitting in an easy chair reading a book.

"Come have a seat," he said pleasantly. "Tell us all about this library."

The teenagers took a seat and each took part in giving the details of the library.

"We thought it would be neat to dedicate the library to the people who built the house," Steve said.

"What a nice thought," the man said. "My father, James actually built the house and then we lived in it until all of our children were grown and it got to be too big for just the two of us. We decided to move into a condo so that we would not have to worry about the upkeep."

"Is the furniture left in the house yours?" Stephanie asked.

They explained that they didn't have room for all of the furniture so they gave some of it to the new owners.

"Was the old roll-top desk yours?" Stephanie asked.

"You mean they left that?" Debbie asked immediately. "I only gave that to Mrs. Smith because she loved it so much."

When Stephanie replied that it was still there, Charlie and Debbie both looked upset.

"That is a valuable desk," Charlie said. "We were going to give it to our daughter, Andrea, but didn't have a way to move it."

"Maybe we should try to get it to her," Debbie said. "I think she was a little upset that we gave it away in the first place but she didn't want to say anything."

Tyler and Steve volunteered to move the desk using their dad's pickup truck.

"That would be super," Charlie said and offered to pay them, but the boys politely refused.

As Charlie was writing down the address of their daughter, Stephanie asked Mr. and Mrs. Essex if they knew anything about a journal with a green velvet cover.

"Do you have it with you?" Charlie quickly asked.

Stephanie pulled out the velvet book from her purse and Charlie's eyes got big when he saw it.

"That book used to belong to my grandmother!" he exclaimed.

Kamryn

Chapter 8
Followed!

Charlie took a few minutes to look over the journal to make sure it was the same book that he was thinking of.

"This is the book that my grandmother used to write in every night after dinner," he added, as he thumbed through the pages.

"I was very little but I remember her writing in the book sometimes when I was visiting," he said.

"So the Charlie in the book isn't you, it's your grandfather," Tyler said.

"Correct," Mr. Essex answered.

"What was your grandmother's name?" Stephanie asked.

"It was Elizabeth, a very beautiful and loving woman," he said showing her his grandmother's picture.

Charlie's grandmother had a very gentle and kind look about her. She had long blond hair that she had pulled up in a French twist and she was wearing an elegant purple dress with a pearl necklace.

"She is beautiful," Stephanie said.

Charlie looked a little sad when he handed the book back to Stephanie.

"Don't you want it?" Stephanie asked.

"Do us a favor and give it to our daughter when you see her," Debbie answered for her husband.

The teenagers promised that they would deliver the journal to Andrea and call her about moving the desk.

"We'll call you after the library is open," Stephanie said. "You should come for the grand opening."

"Well, that solves two mysteries," Tyler said once they were outside.

"Yeah, we now know who built the house and where the diary came from," Stephanie said.

The next day at school, the class voted on naming the library. Essex library won unanimously and upon approval from city council and the school board, it would become their new library name.

"Now I have some more news," Mrs. Adams told the class. "Our book drive was officially over as of yesterday."

Stephanie crossed her fingers and looked in the direction of her brother. Even if they didn't win, she knew that they had given it all their effort and, in the long run, that is what mattered most. When Mrs. Adams announced that the twins were the winners, neither of them knew what to say. They couldn't wait to tell their brother and parents after school.

"Congratulations, Steph. I hope I can help you break in your new tent," Kamryn said, smiling.

"Sure, with summer coming up, we can go on some long camping trips," Stephanie said.

"What's this I hear?" Tyler ran over to where his brother and sister were standing with their friends. "Dylan tells me that you won the tent."

"We sure did, and we couldn't have done it without you," Stephanie said hugging her brother.

"Come on, Steph, stop hugging me, someone might see you," Tyler said.

"Oh, like that would be such a crime," Stephanie teased.

Tyler was about to reply when he got a strange feeling that someone was watching them. Slowly, he turned around and looked towards the woods near the school. He didn't see anyone, but as the trees rustled in the breeze, he got a very uneasy feeling.

No one was at the Thompson house when they got home. A note had been left on the refrigerator.

> We went to Denver to do research on an article. Sorry we didn't tell you sooner. It was last-minute. There is a casserole in the refrigerator for dinner. We will be home late.
>
> Love, Mom and Dad.

"Good, Mom made dinner," Tyler said as he took the casserole out of the refrigerator and put it in the microwave. It took him only a few minutes to eat his

75

dinner and run out the back door with his life vest and rafting gear, leaving his brother and sister to finish eating.

After dinner, Stephanie called the Essex's daughter, Andrea Crum, and introduced herself as a friend of her parents. After talking with her for several minutes, she asked if she would be home the next night.

"Yes, I do plan on being home," Mrs. Crum answered with a confused tone in her voice.

"My brothers and I have a surprise to deliver to you," Stephanie answered. "If it's all right with you, we would like to wait to tell you what and show it to you."

Mrs. Crum, who had gone to school with Stephanie's mother, agreed to wait to be surprised. Although she didn't know much about the Thompson family, she respected them and knew that whatever the surprise was, it could only be good.

Since the weather was so nice, Stephanie and Steve decided to do their homework on the back porch.

"Hi, Sammy, how are you doing?" Stephanie asked their dog who was wagging his tail.

They took turns playing catch with their dog before they decided to do their homework. Sammy lay down beside them and took a nap. He was the first one that heard the garage door opening. He woke up and started barking. Soon their parents appeared and Sammy calmed down.

"You're home early," Stephanie said. "Did you get the research done that you needed?"

"We were hoping that we could do all of the research without taking any books out of the Denver library, but we ran out of time," their mother answered.

"And we did enough work for one day," their father added as he hugged his wife.

"Hey, how about some ice cream?" their mother asked the kids. Even though the question was directed at the teenagers, their father was the first to respond.

"Yeah! That sounds good!" he said, smiling.

"Guess what happened to us today?" Stephanie said, smiling at her parents.

"You got an A on a math test?" Mr. Thompson teased his daughter, whose worst subject was math.

"No," Stephanie said. "We won the book drive contest."

"That's great, honey," Mrs. Thompson said. "We knew that you would win it."

As the family ate their ice cream on the porch, they talked about their upcoming summer plans. Tyler soon walked in the door and joined them.

"Boy, that was fun," he told everyone. He had taken a liking to white water rafting last summer during a camping trip along the Gunnison River and he made it a point to enjoy his hobby every chance he got.

"Well, I think we have all had enough fun for one night," Mrs. Thompson told her children. "It's time for bed."

The next night, the six of them jumped in Mr. Thompson's truck to pick up the desk. The boys were happy that Dylan and Andrew were with them to help move the heavy desk.

Reaching Andrea Crum's house, Stephanie and Kamryn went to the door first.

"We brought your surprise but you have to close your eyes while we bring it in," Stephanie told her.

Once they got the desk inside, Mrs. Crum uncovered her eyes. She didn't say anything right away.

"So what do you think?" Stephanie asked.

"Why it looks just like a desk that once belonged to my great-grandparents," she said.

"It's the same desk," Tyler told her and then went on to explain the whole story of how they had met her parents.

Mrs. Crum loved the desk and was more than grateful; she offered them each a piece of cake. "I thought I would never see that desk again," she told them. "When my parents moved into their condo, I was living in Chicago, and the woman who bought our house loved the desk so much that my parents decided just to let her have the desk."

"Lucky for you, we were trying to find out who built the house where the library is going," Steve said.

"What house are you talking about?" Andrea asked.

"The old colonial house up on Rampart Hill that used to belong to your parents. That's where the library is going." Stephanie said.

"Why, that's the house I grew up in!" Andrea

said,surprised. "I didn't know they were putting a library in there."

"We have been trying to find out who built the house so that we can name the library after them," Kamryn went on to explain.

"And now we can name it Essex Library since we know who built the house," Andrew said.

After they had explained about the library and meeting her parents, Stephanie brought up the journal.

"I have another surprise for you," she said, smiling. "We found something else that belonged to your great-grandmother."

Stephanie pulled out the velvet-covered journal and handed it to Andrea.

"We understand from your father that it belonged to his grandmother," Steve said.

"My great-grandmother," Andrea said, her eyes lighting up. She looked closer at the journal .

"I've enjoyed reading it and now it's even better that I know where it came from," Stephanie said.

Andrea told Stephanie that she could continue reading it if she wanted to.

"That would be great," Stephanie said. She had secretly been sad about giving the journal back because she wasn't finished reading it. "It is so interesting."

"Let me know if there is anything I can do for you to help get the library started," Andrea told the teenagers as they were leaving.

They jumped back into Mr. Thompson's truck. Tyler drove with Stephanie and Kamryn in the front while Dylan, Andrew, and Steve sat in the bed of the truck. Tyler had only driven a few blocks when Dylan noticed a pickup truck that seemed to be following them. He looked closer to see that the man who was driving looked like the man they had seen at the old house!

Andrew

Chapter 9
Some Answers

Frantically, Dylan tried to get Tyler's attention as he knocked on the window between the bed of the truck and the cab. He nodded his head, trying to tell Tyler about the truck following them. Unfortunately, Tyler didn't understand and yelled out the window to ask Dylan what he was saying. Now, it was too late, the driver of the truck had seen that Dylan had noticed him following them and had turned down a side street.

"That's the man we saw at the house. He was in that black pickup truck following us," Dylan yelled.

Tyler drove back to the street that the truck had turned down but it was too late, the driver was nowhere in sight.

As he dropped Dylan and Andrew off, the teens discussed why the man would be following them.

"Maybe he's worried that we might have found whatever he was looking for," Steve said.

"But how did he know where we were?" Stephanie asked.

"He must have followed us from the old house when we picked up the desk," Tyler said.

The teenagers drove around the area for a while,

but it was apparent that the man was nowhere in sight, so they returned home.

Arriving home the Thompson kids went straight up to Tyler's room. His room was at the far west corner of the house facing the mountains. Lately, it had become their meeting room.

"We have to find out who that man is and what he is up to," Stephanie said.

"Yeah, what is he going to do after the library is open, scare all of the kids away?" Steve added.

The three of them sat in silence for a few minutes and then Tyler got an idea.

"I think one of us should go back to see the Smiths and ask them if they know why their son would be snooping around the house," he said.

The three teenagers drew straws, and Steve was elected to go. The next day after church, Tyler dropped him off at the Smith house and waited outside.

When Mrs. Smith answered the door, she was surprised to see the boy again.

"Hi, how can I help you?" she asked.

"Sorry to drop in on you, but the last time we were here we asked you about a photograph that you have hanging near your door," Steve said.

"Yes, I remember. It was a photograph of my son," Mrs. Smith said.

"Well, it's just that we have been working on the library at your old house, and we have seen some one that looks just like your son snooping around," Steve continued.

"Oh, it couldn't be my son, he doesn't live around here," Mrs. Smith replied. "The last I heard, he lived in California."

"Where in California does he live?" Steve asked. "I have an aunt and uncle who live right outside of Los Angeles."

"I don't remember what the town is called, Santa something or other," Mrs. Smith replied.

Steve thanked Mrs. Smith and went back to tell Tyler what he had learned.

"She says that her son lives in California, although she didn't seem too sure about that," Steve told his brother.

"What do you mean?" Tyler asked.

"Well, she said that the last she had heard he lived in California and then she couldn't remember the name of the town," Steve explained.

"It doesn't sound like they have a very good relationship," Tyler commented.

"That's for sure," Steve said. "I also think that there is still a good chance that the man is Chip Smith."

Tyler only nodded in agreement.

Arriving home the two brothers told their sister about Steve's conversation with Mrs. Smith before they sat down to dinner with their family. After dinner the family had a Bible study, which was a week-ly routine for the family every Sunday night. Normally, the teenagers would go to bed shortly after family time, but tonight they got to stay up.

"No school tomorrow!" Stephanie said, yawning. "I love teacher conferences."

"Oh, I forgot to tell you guys, I rented a movie today," Tyler told his brother and sister. "Do you want to watch it with me?"

After Tyler told them about the movie, the twins both agreed that it sounded interesting and after pop-ping some popcorn, they sat down to watch the movie.

The next day they each spent time with their friends doing their favorite things. The boys went fishing but didn't catch anything, and Stephanie and Kamryn went shopping at the mall. After browsing through the music store, the girls went on to the clothes shops.

"That would look really good on you," Kamryn told Stephanie when she picked out a summer short set.

"Yeah, I think I'll try it on," Stephanie said. "I can't believe how close summer is."

Stephanie tried on the outfit and loved the way that it looked on her, so she decided to buy it. Soon it was time for Kamryn's mother to pick them up, so the girls bought sodas and waited near the entrance.

On Tuesday Mrs. Adams told her class about the surprise outing they would have for the whole day.

"As you know, the new library will be opening soon, and the library staff needs help to get it ready," she said. "So today we are going to do our part and pitch in wherever they need us to get the library ready to open.

When everyone cheered at the idea of getting out of class, Mrs. Adams told them it wasn't going to be all fun and games.

"It's hard work to catalog books and it's very important that we take our time going through the books," she said.

Still, it was something different for the kids to do, and they were excited. Before they left for the library, Stephanie told her teacher, Mrs. Adams, about their visit with Andrea Crum when they delivered the desk.

"She is so nice," she told her teacher.

"Maybe you can write a biography about her family to hang on the wall in the library," Mrs. Adams suggested.

Stephanie thought that was a great idea and said she would start right away. She told Kamryn about Mrs. Adams' idea as they got on the bus.

"That's a great idea," Kamryn said. "You'll do a great job."

"Thanks," Stephanie said, smiling.

When they reached the library, the class soon

found out that their teacher wasn't kidding. Books were piled everywhere waiting to be catalogued and then shelved.

The head librarian, Mrs. Williams, introduced herself to the class and set them up in groups to work on the books. Stephanie and Kamryn's group logged the books into the computer and then put the cards in the backs of the books. Steve, Andrew, and Jimmy were assigned the task of placing the books on the shelves.

"I guess this is better than being in school all day," Andrew said.

Jimmy didn't comment but nodded that he agreed.

After school the next day, Stephanie found her older brother and asked him to drive her back to Mrs. Crum's.

"I want to ask her more questions about her family for the biography that I am writing," Stephanie said.

"Sorry, Steph, I have baseball practice" Tyler told his sister.

"I can drive you, Steph," Dylan, who was standing next to Tyler, said. "It's right on my way."

"Thanks, Dylan," Tyler said as he ran off.

Kamryn wanted to come along also, so Dylan dropped Stephanie and Kamryn off at Mrs. Crum's.

"Tell Mom that I'll call home when I need to be picked up," Stephanie told Steve.

Mrs. Crum was delighted to see the girls again.

"It's been a long time since I've had this much company," she told the girls.

When they told her why they stopped in, she smiled even more.

"I would love to tell you about our family," she said, and then went on to tell them almost everything that she knew about her grandparents and her great-grandparents.

Just like the diary had said, her great-grandparents had moved from Kansas to Oro City, which was now a part of Leadville, Colorado. Charlie was a well-known blacksmith and had established customers from all around. It was around the time of the big silver boom when Andrea's grandfather was born.

"This is so cool," Stephanie said after hearing the story. "When I was reading the journal, there was so much that I wanted to know: what the people were like and who the baby was. Now, I have all my answers."

"Our teacher suggested that we include some pictures to hang in the library," Kamryn told Andrea.

"I have lots of pictures," she told them. "Would you girls like something to drink while I get them?"

After pouring three glasses of lemonade, Andrea left the room to look for the pictures. Unfortunately, she soon returned empty handed.

"I forgot that I buried the pictures in the back of the closet," she said.

"That's okay, my mom is probably starting to wonder where I am anyhow," Kamryn said.

"Yeah, it's getting late," Stephanie added. "I'll call home and have Tyler come pick us up."

On their way home, Tyler passed the old house, but there were no lights on this time.

"Well, it doesn't look like that man is there tonight," Stephanie commented.

After Tyler passed the new library, he stopped and backed up a few feet.

"Look, the pickup that was following us is parked in the back," he said.

Tyler was right. In the back of the house, they could see a black pickup truck only partially hidden in the trees. Tyler parked the truck on the side of road where it was hidden by some trees, and the three quietly crept up to the house. They didn't see anyone in the house as they peeked in the windows. After a few minutes of looking around, Tyler motioned them back to the truck.

"It might be too dangerous for us to investigate any further," Tyler said.

After dropping Kamryn off, they headed for home. As they walked in the door, Mrs. Thompson told Stephanie that Mrs. Bradley, Steve's English teacher last year, had called to say that she had found some books.

"She said that you kids could come by tomorrow to pick them up," Mrs. Thompson said.

"Great, even though the book drive is over, we can

still use more books," Stephanie said.

"I can't drive you, Steph, I have baseball practice again tomorrow night," Tyler said.

"We have practice tomorrow night too," Steve spoke up.

"I can pick you up after school and bring you to Mrs. Bradley's," Mrs. Thompson told Stephanie. "I was planning on going to the library to do some research for an article I am writing anyway. Would you like to come along?"

Stephanie, who enjoyed going to the library, quickly agreed to go with her mother.

At Mrs. Bradley's the next day, Stephanie told her about meeting Charlie and Debbie Essex and the diary that Charlie's grandmother had written.

"So we are naming the library Essex Library, and I am writing a biography about their lives to hang in the library."

"What a great idea," Mrs. Bradley said. "You always were a good writer."

At the library, Mrs. Thompson did research for her article while Stephanie started writing the biography. They stayed at the library until closing time.

"I am sorry that it is so late," Mrs. Thompson said.

Stephanie didn't mind because she had gotten a lot written.

"That's okay, but I am starving," she said.

Arriving home, they found their father and

brothers making hamburgers for dinner. So they made a couple of hamburgers for themselves along with some baked onion rings.

"It looks like your mom and I are going to spend most of the weekend at the library," Jack Thompson said. "Do you kids have anything planned?"

"Haven't thought much about it, Dad," Tyler said.

"I'd like to go fishing again," Steve said. "It sure was disappointing on Monday."

"That's a good idea," Tyler said. "Let's call Dylan and Andrew and see if they want to go with us."

But when they called them, they found out that they already had plans to go out with their parents.

"That's okay, we'll still have fun," Tyler told his brother.

When Saturday arrived, Tyler and Steve were up early for a big breakfast before they went fishing.

"I hope the fish are biting," Steve said.

"They better be, I'm counting on you two to bring back dinner," their mother said.

After breakfast the boys got together their tackle boxes and fishing poles and brought the lunch that their mother had made for them.

"I think Sammy wants to come with us," Steve commented as they put their gear in the truck.

Sammy barked as if he knew exactly what Steve had said. The brothers decided to take Sammy with them, hoping that he would not scare the fish away.

This time the brothers went to Nichols Lake

where they almost always brought home fish. It was a long drive and a good hike down to the lake, but it always seemed to be worth it. This trip proved to be no different. It wasn't long before they were reeling in the fish. The day seemed to fly by and it was dark before they started driving home.

"Boy, we sure caught a lot today," Steve said.

"We sure did," Tyler started to say as they drove past the library site. "But maybe we just caught the biggest catch of our day yet."

"What do you mean?" Steve asked.

"Just look up there," Tyler said pointing behind the house. "That man is up there, and he is digging in the backyard!"

Chapter 10
The Key

It wasn't until they had parked their father's truck on the side of the road that they noticed the suspicious man wasn't alone.

"Look, there is another man standing behind Chip!" Steve whispered.

"It looks like the man that ran into me when I ran back into the pizza parlor, and it looks like they are arguing," Tyler exclaimed.

"What should we do?" Steve whispered back.

"Let's try to get closer so we can hear what they are saying," Tyler said.

The boys started to move closer but at that moment Sammy started barking and gave them away. The two men looked up from where they were standing, startled by the noise. By now the two brothers were close enough to hear what they were saying.

"Come on, you idiot," the tall, dark-haired man told Chip. "I knew that you were lying anyway."

The two men didn't say anything else before they disappeared into the woods. Steve started to follow them, but his older brother pulled him back.

"We don't know how dangerous they might be," he warned. "We better not follow them."

"Let's go, Sammy," Steve told his yellow lab, who was still wagging his tail and eyeing the woods. "The fun is over."

They got back in the truck and headed for home.

"What do you think they were looking for, anyhow?" Steve asked.

"I don't know, but they were definitely hiding something or they wouldn't have run away," Tyler answered as they headed for home.

When the brothers arrived home, their mother was in the kitchen making dinner.

"It looks like you boys did really well," she said when she saw the fish they had caught.

"Yeah, and fishing is a lot more fun when you're actually catching some," Steve said.

After cleaning their fish, the brothers went upstairs to find their sister reading.

"You will never guess what we saw today," they told her.

"A big fish jumped out of the water," Stephanie answered, more interested in her book.

But when the brothers told her about the men digging behind the library site, they immediately got her attention.

"I bet they were looking for a trunk," Stephanie said.

"Why do you say that?" Steve asked.

"Just listen to this," Stephanie said as she picked up the journal and started to read.

Gold has been discovered! Charlie and his friends are getting in on buying a claim that has already produced large quantities of gold. The men work day and night digging and guarding the mine from claim jumpers and Ute Indians. Last night a group of Ute Indians took the lives of several miners not far from where Charlie was. I worry for his life and pray for his safety. It is not worth him dying for a few ounces of gold. Yet, Charlie is stubborn and determined to strike it rich and says he wouldn't let a bunch of Indians stop him.

"Dinner is ready," Carol Thompson called up the stairs.

"We'll be right down," Tyler called. "Stephanie, what are you getting at?"

"I'm almost done reading," she answered.

Robberies in the area have been wide spread also. Some people come around begging for food, and I share what I have but I won't let someone come in here and just take because of their greed. I have made sure that my trunk with my treasures is secure and the key is hidden where no one can find it.

"So the trunk is full of treasures," Tyler said as the teenagers went downstairs to dinner.

"Maybe Andrea Crum can tell us what happened to the trunk," Stephanie said.

"That's a good idea, Steph," Tyler said. "Maybe we can stop by her house tomorrow after school."

The twins met Tyler and Dylan after school the next day. After the Thompson kids told their friends about their investigation, everyone was excited to talk with Andrea.

"Do you think Andrea would mind if we all went to her house?" Andrew asked.

"She is so nice. I think she would be happy to see all of us," Stephanie said.

They soon found out that Stephanie was right when Andrea greeted them with a big smile.

"Well, if it isn't the happy six," she said, inviting them in. "What brings you kids by?"

"I found out something very interesting when I was reading the journal last night," Stephanie told Andrea. "Your great-grandmother wrote that she had a trunk where she used to hide all of her valuable possessions. We wondered if you knew anything about it?"

"I think I remember my parents saying that it got lost in one of their moves. I have a vague memory of seeing it once and my mother telling me that it was very old," Andrea told the kids. "I'm glad that you kids are here, I wanted to show you something."

They followed her into her study where they saw the desk immediately.

"It looks really fabulous in here," Stephanie said.

Mahogany bookcases surrounded the room with the desk in the middle. In the far-left corner there was another desk with a computer and printer on it.

"I use this desk as my writing desk," she told the kids.

"Speaking of writing," Stephanie said. "I brought a copy of the biography that I wrote. I was hoping that you would read it for me and tell me what you think, I will be using it for a speech."

"Sure, and that reminds me about those family pictures that I promised you," Andrea said. "I have them ready."

While Andrea went to get the pictures, the teenagers continued to admire the desk.

"Look, it has all kinds of hidden drawers," Steve said as he looked closely at the desk.

"You're right," Tyler said, examining it.

"Maybe the key that Elizabeth mentioned in her diary is hidden in one of the drawers," Dylan suggested.

They looked through every hidden drawer that they could find but didn't come up with anything.

"What about underneath the desk?" Andrew asked.

Upon examining the desk closely, Tyler found what looked like a hidden drawer underneath the desk.

"It looks like this could be a hidden drawer but it won't budge," he told them.

"Let me look," Dylan said.

It took a few minutes, but between the two boys they managed to get the drawer open.

"It looks like we found something," Tyler said.

"An old fashioned key that could be for an old trunk!" Stephanie exclaimed as Tyler held up a key.

Chapter 11
The Final Clue

Finding the key to the trunk was exciting but the teenagers were frustrated because they still had to find the trunk. Andrea called her parents to see if they knew what had happened to the trunk but they couldn't even remember when they had last seen it.

The next day at school, everyone was excited about the Grand Opening of Essex Library, which was to take place the very next day. They had worked so hard getting the library ready for opening day. That night Mrs. Adam's class made sure everything was ready.

"Are you ready to present the biography that you wrote?" Mrs. Adams asked Stephanie.

"Yes, I have it all planned out and Charlie Essex has agreed to say a few words about his parents," Stephanie replied.

"It's too bad we couldn't find the trunk with Elizabeth's belongings. It would have made a great showcase for the opening," Kamryn added.

Mrs. Adams felt that all the kids had done a great job and commended them for their effort.

"You found out who built the house and that is the important thing," she told them.

Class was let out early the next afternoon for the Grand Opening. Mrs. Adams had a bus available to take the whole class to the new library.

Even though Stephanie had organized her whole speech on index cards she was still nervous. The city and school boards were there, the local press, and the Essex family. When Stephanie was done giving her speech, Charlie Essex got up on the stage that they had put together for the special occasion. Stephanie joined her class to listen to what Mr. Essex had to say. As she sat down, she noticed Steve trying to get her attention. She was wondering what she had done wrong until she realized that he wanted her to look toward the back of the room. As she turned her head for a quick glance she saw that Chip Smith was sitting in the back row.

"What was he doing here?" she wondered.

During the dedication, the twins were presented with the tent that they had won for bringing in the most books for the book drive. When the program was over, many people came over to Stephanie to congratulate her on her well-done speech.

Tyler came by the library later with Dylan.

"How did the dedication go?" He asked his brother and sister.

"Everyone I talked to seemed to like my speech," Stephanie said.

"But Chip Smith was hanging around," Steve went on to tell his brother.

"Was he acting strange or did he say anything?" Tyler asked.

"No, he just sat in the back row, but he didn't seem too happy," Steve said.

"Maybe he's just angry because his family lost the house," Tyler said.

"That could be," his brother replied as they started to leave the library.

"Shouldn't we help Mrs. Adams clean up?" Stephanie asked her brothers.

Mrs. Adams gratefully accepted their help. "There is not that much to clean up, and the six of you are quite a team," she said smiling. "With all of us working it shouldn't take very long to clean up."

Andrea decided to stay and help the teenagers clean up also. She helped Stephanie and Kamryn in the kitchen, putting away refreshments, cleaning the coffee urn, and picking up all the paper plates and napkins.

Steve and Andrew moved the chairs back upstairs to a room they used for storage. Tyler and Dylan moved empty boxes back to a spare closet. As Tyler was putting the boxes in the closet, he noticed that the back paneling was a little loose.

"Dylan, could you ask Stephanie if there is a hammer and some nails around here so I can fix this closet," Tyler asked his friend.

After Dylan had left to find the nails, Tyler realized that the closet didn't need fixing after all. The paneling was supposed to be loose because behind it was a narrow staircase. Tyler climbed the narrow stairs to find a big attic.

"Tyler, where are you?" Dylan called when he came back to the closet to find that his friend had disappeared.

"I'm up here," Tyler called back. "There's a tiny staircase behind the paneling in the closet."

Dylan moved to the back of the closet and saw what Tyler meant. He started climbing up the stairs when Steve came over.

"What's going on?" he asked.

"We found a staircase," Dylan said.

"That's not all we found!" Tyler called back. "Dylan, come up here, I need your help with this trunk."

As the two boys lugged the heavy trunk down the stairs, Stephanie and Kamryn came over to see what all the noise was about.

"You found the trunk!" Stephanie exclaimed.

"Hey, that's my trunk!" Chip Smith said as he unexpectedly walked into the hallway.

"What do you mean it's your trunk?" Tyler asked him angrily. "Your initials are C. S. and this trunk is initialed E. E. Those are not your initials."

"Those initials are my grandmother's, Edna Englewood, her maiden name," the man said.

"Oh, really. Can you prove it?" Stephanie asked.

"I shouldn't have to," the man said.

"Do you have the key?" Kamryn asked Chip.

As Chip pulled out a large old-fashioned key that looked like it could possibly fit the trunk, a tall dark-haired man suddenly appeared behind the teenagers.

"It doesn't matter who has the key, because that trunk is mine," the man said, looking straight at Chip. "And it better have some real jewels inside or you'll be worse off than Harry."

The teenagers stood there in silence as they listened to the two men fight over the trunk. It wasn't long before they were in a tug of war fighting over it. The two men were so busy arguing that they didn't notice Steve slip out the back door to go for help.

Steve ran as fast as he could to the main road. He hoped that he would see someone drive by before he reached the Simms' house, which was the closest house around. He soon discovered he was in luck when he saw a car coming. As the car got closer, it slowed down, and Steve was pleasantly surprised to see his parents.

"What are you guys doing here?" he asked.

"We got to thinking about that strange man who has been hanging out at the house," his mother began.

"Mom, you don't have to say anymore." Steve said, hugging his mother. "For once, I'm really glad that you're a little overprotective."

"What's wrong, son?" Jack Thompson asked.

"I'll explain on the way," Steve said. "Right now we need Officer Morton."

While the family headed for the police department, the teens were back at the library trying to put together some of the missing pieces of the mystery.

"It's my guess that you have been searching everywhere for this trunk. What I don't understand is why you were looking in the cupboards in the kitchen?" Tyler said to Chip.

"He was probably trying to throw you off the trail," the man standing next to Chip said. "He told me that the trunk was buried somewhere in the backyard."

"I was just guessing, I didn't know for sure," Chip answered. "And as far as the kitchen goes, it's none of your business what I was looking for."

"Could it had been this?" Stephanie asked pulling out the green velvet journal from her purse.

"The diary! Where did you find it?" Chip asked.

"Easy, your mother gave it to us, just like she gave your identity away!" Stephanie answered. "How can you let her think that you live somewhere in California anyway?"

Before Chip had a chance to say anything, the other man spoke up.

"He might not be in California right now, but he is going back with me," the man said. "That way, when Harry gets out of jail, he can pound your head in."

"Who is Harry?" Andrew asked.

"He and Butch, here, robbed a liquor store and I was a witness against them." Chip said. "My testimony put Harry in jail."

"Oh shut up!" the man yelled at Chip. "You know darn well that you had as much to do with that robbery as we did."

As the man said this, the Buena Vista Police Department was closing in on the two men. Luckily, there were two entrances into the library so the police could sneak in behind the men. Steve was playing decoy and came in the front entrance and then made sure that the men saw him standing in the doorway. Their plan worked just the way they wanted.

"And where do you think you're going?" Butch asked. "We don't need you kids trying to pull anything."

Before he had even finished talking the police had grabbed him and Chip from behind.

"That sounded like a threat," an officer said. "What do you think, Officer Morton?"

"I think these men might need to take some time to think about their actions," Officer Morton said.

"You might want to check with California to see if they are wanted there," Tyler said. "We know they were at least involved in one robbery."

"Hey, we never threatened anyone, and as far as the trunk goes, it belongs to Chip," the man named Butch said.

"Oh, yeah, prove it," Steve challenged.

Chip just stood there and didn't say anything.

"Go ahead, open it with your key," Butch ordered.

Chip tried to use the key to open the lock but it was obvious that it didn't fit.

"This is the right key, Officer" Andrea said. "My great grandmother hid it in a very old desk that she had."

She pulled the key from her purse and started to open the trunk.

"It doesn't sound like you have much of a case," one of the officers was saying to Chip when Tyler pulled an old photo album out of the trunk."

"I suppose these are photographs of your relatives?" Tyler said to Chip, showing him the album.

"That's right," Chip mumbled.

"Oh, look, Andrea. Here is a photograph from your great grandparents' wedding," Tyler said as he turned to Andrea.

As the teenagers and the police looked through the photo album, they could see that it was all from Andrea's family. There was even a group of photos labeled "Essex Family Reunion."

"This trunk clearly belongs to this woman," the officer in charge said. "Now, if you will come with us, we have some more questions to ask you."

"You can't arrest us, we didn't do anything wrong!" Chip said.

"Maybe you didn't commit any crime here but I understand you boys helped rob a liquor store," Officer Morton said.

"You and your big mouth," Butch said to Chip.

Officer Morton thanked the teenagers again before leaving and told them he would let them know what they found out about the two men's involvement in the robbery.

"I can't believe that Chip would go to the trouble of making up that whole story, just to get these things," Tyler said as he looked through the trunk. "This stuff has more sentimental value than monetary value."

"That's just it," Stephanie said. "In the journal, Elizabeth writes that she has put all her treasures in the trunk. He thought that she meant things that could be very valuable, but she meant her sentimental treasures."

"And with Butch breathing down his neck about busting his friend, he had to come up with something," Steve said.

"I'm glad we were able to find the trunk for you, Andrea," Stephanie said.

"I can't tell you how grateful I am," Andrea said as she looked through the trunk. "You kids did such a good job solving this mystery."

"Yeah, we were good detectives," Steve said.

The Thompson kids didn't know it yet but this was only the first of many mysteries that the young detectives would solve. Soon they would have a whole new adventure in Manitou Springs, where they would solve the ***Manitou Art Caper.***

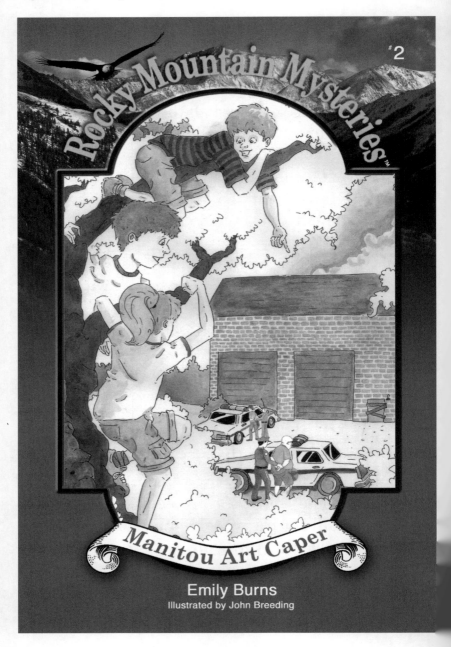

Read a section of our next book, <u>Manitou Art Caper!</u>

A few minutes later two men walked out of Aunt Marybeth's gallery. They got in the pickup truck and talked for a few minutes. As the truck pulled away from the curb, one of the men looked right in the direction of the teenagers. Tyler was certain the men had seen them, but decided to continue following them in his car. He was staying close behind when all of a sudden a large truck pulled out from nowhere.

"Look out!" Stephanie yelled.

Check it out!

Our website address is:
RockyMountainMysteries.com

- Be the first to know what titles in the series are coming next.

- Find out where you can meet the author and get a book signed.

- Get to know more about the characters in the books.

- Learn historical facts about the Rocky Mountain region.

- Check out our fun stuff link. It's loaded with puzzles and trivia.

- Link to other cool websites.

- Plus, special chat times will be set up to talk with the author!

- And, keep checking back as we will be adding to and updating our website often!

A Brief History
of the Rocky Mountains

There is something about the Rocky Mountains that no words can fully describe. The Rockies extend from New Mexico through Colorado, Utah, Idaho, Wyoming, and into Canada. With the sheer peaks also come desert sands, mountain lakes, beautiful wildflowers, and a colorful history.

Researchers continue to find evidence of prehistoric habitation. The Anasazi people, perhaps the first inhabitants, are known for their stone masonry displayed in the cliff dwellings at Mesa Verde National Park near Cortez, Colorado. Next, came the Indian tribes: the Arapahoe, Cheyenne, and Ute, to name only a few. The Spanish would soon join them and bring with them horses and tools, changing their lives.

The prospectors came in the 1860's, hoping to strike it rich. Some of them were bound for California, and for them the Rockies were just an obstacle in their way. Many would later wish that they had stopped in Colorado where gold was discovered in 1858.

One of the places where prospectors hoped to find gold was Oro City. Today, it is a part of Leadville, Colorado. There, the miners would discover that black sand was clogging their boxes, making it hard to produce the gold ore. It wasn't until 1875 when two miners, William Stevens and A.B. Wood, would rework the mines to realize that the black sand had a high amount of silver. From that point on Oro City, now Leadville, became one of the richest cities in the state. By 1880, it was the second largest city in Colorado.

With the mining industry came the need for lumber, railroads, and community services. Eventually, the mines would run out or the market would fail. Today, we are left with ghost towns to remind us of the area's rich history.

Autobiography of
Emily Burns

Emily Burns was only four years old the first time she saw the Rocky Mountains and fell in love with them. Growing up in Ohio, she dreamed that someday she would make her home in the mountains, and as she grew up, she realized another passion: writing. Even as a young child, she could often be found in some hidden corner writing or reading.

Having spent a lot of time with children, including work as a nanny, Emily has come to realize that writing for children is an area that comes naturally for her. In particular, she excels in writing mysteries for juveniles, which is still her favorite reading material even as an adult.

Today, she resides in Aurora, Colorado, just east of the mountains, with her daughter and husband.

Artist Bio

John Breeding is a talented young artist currently studying fine arts at his high school in Colorado. His artwork has appeared in many art shows, and he has received the Outstanding Young Authors and Illustrators Award. His plans for the future include college and a career in art.

Give the Gift of

Rocky Mountain Mysteries™

to your children, relatives, friends, or anyone with kids 8-12 years old
Check Your Local Bookstore or Order Here

☐ *Mystery on Rampart Hill* _____ x $4.95 = _____

☐ *Manitou Art Caper* _____ x $4.95 = _____

☐ *Marked Evidence* _____ x $4.95 = _____
Available March 2003

Add $2.00 shipping for one book
plus $1.00 for each additional book = _____

CO Residents add
.18¢ sales tax per book = _____

Total Enclosed = _____
U.S. Funds Only
Please allow up to six (6) weeks for delivery

Name _____

Address _____

City _____ State _____ Zip _____

Phone _____

Email Address _____

Parents:
Fill out to pay by Credit Card or Order online at
www.RockyMountainMysteries.com

Please circle one MasterCard **VISA**

CC Number _____ Exp Date _____

Authorized Name _____

Signature _____

Make Checks or Money Orders payable and mail to:
Covered Wagon Publishing, LLC
P.O. Box 473038
Aurora, CO 80047
(303) 751-0992 Fax (303) 632-6794

Give the Gift of

Rocky Mountain Mysteries™

to your children, relatives, friends, or anyone with kids 8-12 years old
Check Your Local Bookstore or Order Here

☐ ***Mystery on Rampart Hill*** _____ x $4.95 = _____

☐ ***Manitou Art Caper*** _____ x $4.95 = _____

☐ ***Marked Evidence*** _____ x $4.95 = _____
Available March 2003

Add $2.00 shipping for one book
plus $1.00 for each additional book = _____

CO Residents add
.18¢ sales tax per book = _____

Total Enclosed = _____
U.S. Funds Only
Please allow up to six (6) weeks for delivery

Name _____

Address _____

City _____ State _____ Zip _____

Phone _____

Email Address _____

Parents:
Fill out to pay by Credit Card or Order online at
www.RockyMountainMysteries.com

Please circle one MasterCard VISA

CC Number _____ Exp Date _____

Authorized Name _____

Signature _____

Make Checks or Money Orders payable and mail to:
Covered Wagon Publishing, LLC
P.O. Box 473038
Aurora, CO 80047
(303) 751-0992 Fax (303) 632-6794